The

SOCCER

diaries

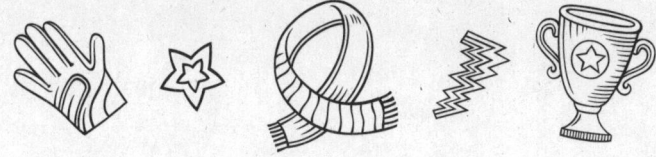

The SOCCER diaries

BOOK 2
ROCKY'S BIG MOVE
by Tom Palmer

REBELLiON

First published 2024 by Rebellion Publishing Ltd,
Riverside House, Osney Mead, Oxford, OX2 0ES, UK

ISBN: 978-1-83786-100-2

10 9 8 7 6 5 4 3 2

A CIP catalogue record for this book is available from the
British Library.

Designed & typeset by Rebellion Publishing
Cover art © Gabriela Epstein, 2023

Printed in Denmark

MIX
Paper | Supporting
responsible forestry
FSC® C104608

To my cousin, Helen McGee, for being there.

1

ROCKY HAD NEVER deployed a Cruyff turn on the football field before.

The Cruyff turn was an offensive move where you tricked your defenders and left them on their backsides. Rocky was not known for offensive moves. For *being* offensive, yes. But not in the football way.

In training that day, her back to the goal, irritated that she had no support and that two defenders, Mahsa and Naomi, were right up behind her, she felt like surprising everyone with a Cruyff turn.

The closest player to her was her best friend,

Kim, but Kim was hobbling, uncomfortable. Rocky guessed she had a dead leg and so was—for the moment—out of the game.

And so, back to goal, Rocky made as if to play the ball infield to Kim. Then, as Naomi moved to follow the ball away from goal and Mahsa backed off, Rocky turned and tapped the ball back towards goal with her heel, twisted her body out of Naomi's reach and followed the ball into the penalty area.

A Cruyff turn, perfectly executed.

Now Naomi was off-balance and Rocky had gained five yards of space. And—with Ella in goal right back on her line, not expecting a shot—Rocky had the angles too. One touch, two touches, she fired it home. Top corner. No chance for Ella.

Even before the ball hit the back of the net, Rocky heard Abby, their coach—and former US international—whooping.

Americans did that. Whooping. It was one of their things. A group of American football players were clapping wildly too.

Rocky had found that a lot of Americans, anyway, were very expressive, whooping, cheering, hollering in the sun. They were far more expressive than any fourteen-year-old girl who'd been brought up in the shadows of the hills in a cold northern English city. The sort of place where you kept your thoughts and emotions deep inside and rarely raised an eyebrow when something amazing or even terrifying happened.

But Rocky would forgive this whooping because she idolised Coach Abby. She had been at this high school in California for a few days and the only thing she really needed right now—not her familiar bedroom at home, not England, not even her mum—was Coach Abby's approval.

And now she had it.

Rocky could not remember feeling so good. This was working out. Really working out! At the age of fourteen she had come to study at a sports high school in the United States of America. And not just in the USA. In California! In Los Angeles. Near Hollywood and Beverly Hills. Close to beaches and surfers and dawn to dusk sunshine. On pitches that were near to perfect, watered every evening after a day in the heat, all overlooked by elegant college buildings lined with palm trees.

Paradise. Perhaps.

And—even better—the whole thing was being paid for by the school. Because… and this was the most amazing thing of all… because they thought she was that good at football. Or soccer. That's what they called it here. Soccer. And that was fine by Rocky, too. They could whoop. She might even whoop.

She would call football 'soccer'. She would call boots 'cleats'. And the benches round the pitch, 'bleachers'. She would call the pitch the 'field'. What did words matter when you were living the dream?

"Where on earth did you learn to do that?" Kim asked, still hobbling, but coming to congratulate Rocky on the goal.

"A Cruyff turn?" Rocky said.

"A what?"

"Cruyff was a Dutch footballer. A man."

"Okay?"

"And he had this trick. You know, like Ronaldo had his stepovers… for what they were worth."

"Like your brother, Roy, has the Rocket?"

"Hmmm. I suppose," Rocky conceded. It was true. Her Premier League-playing brother had a volley that had been nicknamed the Rocket.

"So how do you know about all these moves?"

"I am a student of football. I watch them online. I read about them. I learn."

"Abby was impressed," Kim said. "She looooves you."

"And you."

Kim shrugged. "I've been here three years. You're new."

They walked back to the centre spot in silence.

"One day," Rocky said, "all those moves on YouTube…"

"Yeah?"

"One day they'll be named after women. Not just men like Ronaldo and Cruyff. There might be a Kim Courtney Counterattack or a Rocky Race Reverse. What do you think?"

Kim grinned. "Yes to that," she said.

2

WALKING AWAY FROM the football fields, Rocky and Kim, joined by Mahsa and Naomi, chatted about a big game that was coming up during the week. A friendly. Or scrimmage, as it was known in the States.

They all became distracted at the same time. By noise. Lots of noise. There was drumming, and trumpets and cheering. Up ahead on the bleachers of the first team American football field, hundreds of students were cheering. There were flags and banners, and cheerleaders leaping around.

Rocky—a hater of fuss—felt uneasy, but

Kim, suddenly excited, began to jog over to the football field.

"Come on! It's the Pep Rally! You'll love it," she laughed.

Rocky ran after the others as they approached the field, saw and heard the stamp of feet on the benches. What else could she do? She liked Kim. A lot. She didn't want to be disrespectful to her or the school she'd been at for years.

"Pep who?" Rocky shouted.

"Pep Rally. We welcome the varsity football team and cheer them on!"

It was hard to hear Kim above the noise of a marching band. Rocky—along with Mahsa and Naomi—kept following her. She had another question.

"But why?" Rocky said as they climbed to the back of a stand.

"School spirit!" Kim said, hands above her

head, clapping to the beat the cheerleaders were dancing to as the other three watched.

Rocky raised her hands above her head and joined in. Partly because it was so absurd, but partly because she figured she needed some school spirit and—as Mahsa and Naomi had joined in also—she had to.

And the spirit came. It was really quite strange for her. She could feel the hairs standing up on her arms and the back of her neck. It was a bit like going to see Melchester Rovers at the football. The buzz. The excitement of live sport with a big crowd.

Soon she found herself hugging her three friends and, then, other students she didn't know. Grinning. Laughing.

"Good?" Kim asked, shouting above the noise after a few minutes of mayhem.

"I love it!" Rocky screamed. "I love school spirit!"

After the Pep Rally had died down, Rocky sat with Kim, Mahsa and Naomi on one of several sets of benches for eating, set out on the edge of the playing fields, thirstily taking on water and energy drinks.

It was seven in the evening, late September, but the sun was still very warm. Dozens of other students at the school sat out enjoying the evening. This was another one of the things Rocky had to get used to. Students at Mountain Heights ate most of their meals—and chilled—outside.

She liked this, too.

Rocky took a long drink from her water bottle as she studied the playing fields, well-kept lawns and small clusters of trees that formed a barrier between the sports fields and Mountain Heights School, California.

Was this real? Was she actually sitting here with these other—mostly American—

children? Rocky could still not believe it. This was LA for goodness' sake! A school in LA, and Rocky was a student here! At the kind of school you saw on Netflix dramas or The Kardashians. The school was all bright white plaster and terracotta roof tiles. The light so bright it hurt your eyes as it bounced back off the walls. It reminded Rocky of the one foreign holiday in Greece she and her family had had before she came to the States.

This was so different to post-training in Melchester, back home in England. At this time on a Melchester evening in September it would be fifteen degrees cooler, the wind blowing dead wet leaves at you, or showers of chilling rain and a sky already going dark as she traipsed up the hill of terraced houses that led to her home.

Rocky smiled and took a deep breath. Did she miss all that? Home?

A bit, maybe. She missed her mum. Maybe her brother, Roy. Occasionally. And the cool air and the way that air smells when the leaves are coming off the trees and you sense the first bite of winter. She used to like that.

But there was something about being away from her mum that felt good, too. And avoiding her brother and all the sister–brother tension rubbish. And a town where she felt like everyone knew her and was watching her, even judging her. Like they knew she had done badly at school. Like they only saw her as Roy of the Rovers' sister. Or the daughter of Danny Race who had recently died of cancer. Not a person in her own right. Here, she was anonymous. Here, she was free. Here, she could be who she wanted to be.

Couldn't she?

On the field beside their table and benches were three boys, tossing an American football to each other. Rocky identified them as the same boys who had been watching her girls' soccer squad teammates training.

One of them, Cody, a friend of Kim's and the reason they were there to watch, was looking at Rocky. She had tried to ignore him, but he was persistent.

Rocky turned to Cody. "What?"

"Nice soccer move, English," he said.

"Eh?"

"Nice soccer move, I said."

Rocky took another breath and wondered how to respond. She knew what she was supposed to say. Thank you. Thanks for watching. You're so cool. Blah blah blah. But she thought better of that. Always. She had never been able to cope with the things you were supposed to say.

"Thanks. Kind of you to say. But, for the record, it's football!"

"What?" Cody stopped.

"It's called football," Rocky explained. "I play football."

Looking confused, Cody held up a ball shaped like a rugby ball. "This is a football," he said.

Rocky smiled. She felt the eyes of her friends on her. She wanted to come out of this well, make her friends laugh, but not make Cody feel bad.

"No, no," she grinned. "You play catch."

"What?"

"I'm trying to explain it to you," Rocky went on. "Ask yourself… why do you throw that ball to each other and play catch with it, but still think it is called football?"

Cody had stopped now. "I don't get you."

"I use my foot to play football. You use your hands to play catch."

Rocky could see Cody's friends laughing

at him now. The school's big-deal American football player was being toyed with. She actually felt a bit sorry for him. But again she remembered her brother Roy, also the best sports person at his school. The one everyone worshipped. Boys like this needed help to stay grounded. She could help Cody like she'd helped Roy.

Rocky smiled. "I like you, Cody. Take a few days to think about it, then we'll talk it through, yeah?"

Cody shrugged and jogged to catch up with his friends as they left, pushing each other playfully.

"You know you're not supposed to talk to the varsity guys like that?" Kim said, laughing, reworking her long black hair into a ponytail, tightening it with quick fingers. "You're supposed to blush and go quiet and giggle."

"I'll remember that," Rocky smiled, "next time I see him." Rocky wasn't quite sure if Kim was joking or serious. But she wasn't quite sure about lots of things now she lived in the US.

Rocky did know that that was one of the rules of Mountain Heights High School. That boys who played American football and baseball were at the top of the hierarchy. And soccer players, especially girls, were at the bottom. That it also mattered who your family was and what sort of car you drove and whose party you were invited to, to which clique you belonged and which clique you avoided. She had got all that on day one at Mountain Heights and she had found the rules and the traditions so overwhelming, so overpowering, that she decided not to have anything to do with them.

And why not?

She had experienced and played along with all the games and rules like this before. At school in England, in Melchester. Of course, it was more glamorous and edgy in California, but it was the same everywhere. People wanting you to choose which box to be boxed up in. Accepting you, rejecting you, messing with your head so that their own head stayed safe.

Rocky would have no chance of understanding and playing those games as skillfully—and ruthlessly—as you needed to. No.

So she had made a decision. She would treat people as people and ignore what you were supposed to do, who they were, who they knew, all that nonsense. She would make a point of not following the rules. And if that included winding up catch-a-ball Cody, then fine.

3

Rocky, Kim, Mahsa and Naomi lived together behind one door. A shared living room with a circle of sofas and a large TV screen. A floor-to-ceiling window looked out towards the hills to the north. They also had a balcony where they could sit on chairs and feel the sun on their faces.

It was amazing.

Four en suite bedrooms came off the shared living space. There were no cooking facilities: they ate all three meals in the school cafeteria, a three-minute walk along a corridor, down two flights of stairs and across the quad.

It was perfect. Life was easy. Life was good. Here, Rocky was in a place she loved with three other girls she really really liked.

She looked up to them all in different ways. Naomi was clever and kind. Mahsa was fiery and unpredictable. And Kim… Rocky adored her, had never had a friend like her. Someone she trusted and who trusted her. In fact, that was how it was with all the girls. She knew that they liked and trusted her. Their friendships were easy. They were fun. There was no drama.

This was new to Rocky. And it made her feel good.

The quartet finished the smoothies they'd got from the cafeteria and slumped on the sofas in the middle of their living space. All of them on their mobiles. Or cell phones. That was another Americanism Rocky had to get used to.

Football. Soccer. Mobiles. Cells. Pitches. Fields. There were endless words you could find yourself caught out saying.

"Are we all okay?" Kim asked.

Even though they were all the same age, Kim was the unofficial parent, because she had been at Mountain Heights for years. Rocky, Mahsa and Naomi were all new, freshers, so they were relieved that Kim was happy to be the grownup.

Kim's mum lived close by in a beach house, but was away with work so much that Kim boarded at the school. The other girls' mums were all thousands of miles away. And that was because Mahsa, Naomi and Rocky were all on overseas scholarships.

Mahsa, from Iran, was tall and agile-looking and wore a white headscarf.

Naomi, from Ghana, was tall, too, but stockier. Together she and Mahsa had already formed a fierce central defensive partnership on the pitch.

Being on an overseas scholarship meant that the school coached them, educated them, fed and boarded them all for free. Rocky too.

And why did they get free education, coaching, food, all near the California beach? Why were they living this dream?

Because they were good at football.

It was hard to believe. That her life was good after a couple of years of it being so not good.

And she knew that it had changed last summer when she had travelled to Los Angeles for a two-week chance-of-a-lifetime soccer camp. She had not dreamed it would be anything other than a one-off.

Things had not played out that way.

The soccer camp had been such a success for the school, with Mountain Heights beating teams they had never beaten before. And it had been a surprise success for Rocky: Abby, the school coach, had offered Rocky, Mahsa and Naomi scholarships to play and study at the high school.

After more chatting, the four of them agreeing to have a movie night soon, Mahsa and Naomi walked towards their bedroom doors. It was late now. Time to turn in.

"Good night," Mahsa said. Then Naomi.

Kim turned to Rocky and asked, "You okay?"

"I really am," Rocky beamed. She felt good. Happy. At home here.

"You were funny with Cody earlier," Kim said. "I think he liked it that you had a joke with him. He's probably not used to it."

Rocky frowned. "Was it rude? I mean… was I rude?"

"A bit. But in a funny way. That's what I mean. Some boys can take that, even like it.

Some can't. I think Cody did."

Rocky smiled at Kim. Kim smiled back. And Rocky wondered if she'd ever had a friendship like this before.

"Night, then," she said, closing her door. She didn't put her light on. The sky outside was still glowing bright.

Rocky faced her room and gazed absent-mindedly at her duvet cover and throw she'd bought with her mum at Dunelm back in the UK. The tapestry on the wall she'd ordered online. And the rug that Mum had sent to her as a gift when she arrived in the US from the UK. It was four feet across and round, made of rags tied together.

She had spent hours putting things on the walls, moving the bed to a different angle, sorting her clothes and toiletries and everything else, filling drawers and arranging shelves to make the room into... her room.

Her room.

Her space.

Rocky sat on the rug and crossed her legs, closed her eyes and breathed out a long and deep sigh.

The rug. She focused on the rug.

When she had been little, Rocky's mum had got her a book from the library about a child who travelled the world on a magic carpet. She had never forgotten that book, that feeling. And she riffed off that idea when she sat on Mum's carpet.

But she didn't want to travel the world on her rug. She just wanted to spend a few minutes there thinking.

This rug, for Rocky, was where she could let herself be herself. The deep-down Rocky. The Rocky hidden away from the Cruyff turns and the goading of American boys and a group of girls she loved being with. Where she could worry about things that might undo her.

It had taken a while at Mountain Heights School for Rocky to realise what her thing was. The threat. To everything. It wasn't football. It wasn't friendship. Both of those things were great.

The thing that was not so great?

School work.

4

A MONTH INTO her first term—called semester in the US—at Mountain Heights School, Rocky knew quite well what her problem was.

The football was great. The friendships were great. The movie nights. The chats. Everything except one thing.

She didn't do classrooms.

School had always been a struggle for her. When she was at school in England, being in the classroom felt to her like being chained into a cell with lots of other people chained there too, made to sit and face an adult who was telling you stuff and showing you stuff and sometimes—worst of all—asking you stuff.

When she felt like bouncing off the walls, she had to sit and read and write. And she just couldn't do that when required to at 8.50 a.m., Monday to Friday, for six or seven hours. More, if she got a detention.

Rocky liked to understand things, think about things, talk about things. To learn, yes. But not in a classroom.

But here she was, the California sun streaming in through the blinds. In a classroom. Facing a teacher talking in front of a smart board and posters of key moments from American history, rows of people behind her, in front of her, either side of her, trying really hard to buy into it, but not being able to take a word in of what was being said.

And knowing—but not really facing up to—

the bleak truth that if she did not get a grip in the classroom, she could lose everything. Everything. The school. The new life. The football. The friendship. Because that was the truth. She had to pass end-of-term exams to stay on the scholarship. If she failed, she'd be going home.

Day after day she faced this anxiety. But still, day after day she dodged the teachers' questions and nagging. She kept her head down. Kept the problem at bay. Avoided the scrutiny of her teachers skilfully.

Until a day in mid-October, a month into her scholarship.

"Rocky Race?"

Mrs Achebe, the English Literature teacher, was smiling at her. "Please stop staring out of the window and engage. You never put your hand up, so today I am coming to you. Now, what can you tell us about this book? It's set in England. Can you help us understand it better?"

Rocky snapped to attention. She had, while staring out of the window, been worrying about Kim. Over the last couple of days, Kim had been different with her. And with other people. Rocky was trying to work out what was different and why. She hated it when things were not normal. The friendship and football had to be perfect for her to be able to cope with everything else.

"Which book, Mrs Achebe?" Rocky spluttered. "Sorry. I had my mind on something else."

There was a laugh from the rest of the class. A laugh that was with Rocky, not at her. She hoped.

Mrs Achebe sighed. "Come on, Rocky. We're talking about Wuthering Heights. One of the greatest English books ever written!

By Emily Brontë. We're going to be reading it. It's set on the moors in northern England. It's a love story. Cathy and Heathcliff. Yes?"

Rocky bristled. Why did teachers do that? 'Don't look out of the window' meant 'don't think'. 'Why do you not put your hand up?' And sometimes she was asked why she took too many school notes. Too many! All those things were annoying. And so, frankly, was doing a book set up the road from where she lived in the UK. Yes, she knew the book. Or knew about it. She'd never read it. But she had been to the house where the Brontë sisters had lived. In a place called Haworth. Or was it called Halifax? She had walked on the moors Mrs Achebe was talking about. Run on them. And she could talk about the heather, purple in late summer, as if the moors were embers in a fire, glowing as the sun went down. She also knew about the wind up there, that *wuthering* was the sound that the wind made when it hit your house, a humming, moaning sound that you could imagine was a ghost if you believed that the dead came back to life, which Rocky didn't. In fact, her brother's ex-girlfriend, Ffion, had told her that Wuthering Heights wasn't a love story at all, but about a man trying to control everyone. She had so much she could say, but her mind... her mind was stuck. What was this? Why did this happen? Her mind. Just. Couldn't. Wouldn't. Work. If she had to speak.

Rocky looked up to the front, glanced sidewards at the other children in other chairs at other desks and said, "I don't know anything about it."

She stared down at the stick figures she had drawn on her workbook, aware that Mrs Achebe had quickly typed something into her laptop and pressed send.

What was that? Rocky wondered.

Rocky stared around her. Most of the others in the classroom had looked away now, but Naomi was still studying Rocky, a concerned—or was it confused?—look on her face. Rocky gave her friend a smile to deal with the weirdness.

Naomi smiled back. Rocky thought it was nice to feel like she had an ally in the classroom.

In the distance, outside her head, Rocky could still hear Mrs Achebe's voice. And the voices of other classmates talking about the book. She closed her eyes. There was a buzzing sound in her ears. She wanted so desperately to stand up and walk out of the classroom, along the corridor, out to the football field. But she knew that would make things worse.

What she had to do was do what she had always done: to sit in the classroom and look like she was there. To speak when she was spoken to. To find a way to dodge the attention of the teachers, like a striker trying to lose a defender at a corner kick. Then, when they were dismissed, leave the classroom and come back to life.

This was how she would carry on. Then she could play football and spend time with her friends.

It was a strategy, a gameplan. And it worked. Usually.

But not today. After the bell rang, after class, someone was waiting for her.

Jesse.

The assistant soccer coach. And her school counsellor.

"Rocky," Jesse said. "Mrs Achebe says you've been struggling. We should talk."

"Maybe later?" Rocky suggested.

"Maybe now," Jesse said firmly.

5

"How are you feeling about the game tomorrow?" Jesse asked.

Jesse was not much taller than Rocky. But he did have a huge presence. He was calm and as they walked the school corridors people smiled at him, some high-fiving or fist-bumping him. It meant that Jesse seemed much taller, much more present as they arrived at the coffee and smoothie bar.

"Great," Rocky replied. "I'm feeling great. I always feel great."

She knew what this was. It was Jesse who Mrs Achebe had messaged during class.

This was the follow up.

"Really?" Jesse challenged her.

"You know I am. I am doing great in training, we rock as a team, and Abby seems to like me. It's going to be amazing. I love it. But… that's not what you want to talk to me about, is it?"

"Not entirely." Jesse was smiling.

For a moment Rocky reflected that she had said that her team 'rocked'. It was a phrase she'd never have used in the UK. But it seemed to slip out quite easily now she lived in the US.

And then her mind flipped back to seeing Kim before class. How Kim had been quiet and Rocky couldn't work out why. Since last night she had sensed Kim had been trying to appear normal, but that there was something bugging her. It wasn't like a rift in their friendship, but there was something hurting

Kim. And Rocky wanted to make it better. But first she had to deal with Jesse and the Mrs Achebe thing. Get it out of the way.

Rocky was not used to this. Having a counsellor. Someone delving into her brain. At school in the UK you might have a head of year for your year group, but it wasn't like this. And she still couldn't get her head round the fact a counsellor was there to help her get the best out of school. He wasn't like a therapist, someone who asked you how you were feeling all the time. Although he often did.

Rocky was coming to understand that schools were different in the US than the UK. And that until she understood exactly how they were different she would not feel settled.

So much to deal with.

"You want to talk to me about Mrs Achebe," she said.

"Mrs A says you're struggling," Jesse conceded.

Rocky nodded. "She's right."

They sat down at a table after ordering drinks. Jesse sat opposite Rocky, leaning back, easy in the chair, arms open. Rocky folded her arms and leaned tight into the table.

They had been here before. When Rocky came to the summer camp, Jesse had talked to her, tried to help her. And she liked that. The fact he listened. Had teachers in the UK listened to her, understood her? One or two, but not many. They'd been too busy. But this felt different. But she still folded her arms.

"So, what can I do to help? I'm your learning mentor. It's my job to help you find solutions."

"No offence, Jesse, but I don't like having conversations."

Rocky immediately regretted being rude to him. These reactions just slipped out of her, even to people she liked.

"Talking? You don't like talking? We talked in the summer. Didn't we?"

"Oh, no, I mean I love talking. Just not proper serious conversation talking. Not that endless face-to-face come-and-sit-on-this-couch stuff. It makes me feel weird."

Jesse nodded and studied Rocky across the table.

"See," she complained. "You're doing it now. Even the silences in one of your conversations are agony."

Jesse moved to sit on the chair next to Rocky. "How's this? Not so face-to-face?"

"Weirder," Rocky said.

Jesse moved back to sit opposite Rocky and smiled, staring at the hills. He thought this conversation was funny. She could see that as she stared at the hills, too. But maybe he wasn't allowed to show he was amused.

"You been running up there?" he asked. "I know you like cross country."

Rocky shook her head. "I'd like to. I love running on my own. But there was something online about it not being safe up there. I think a woman was attacked."

Jesse nodded. "I heard that. But it was a while ago. A couple of years. It should be okay now. But maybe run together with someone else?"

"But that's not okay," Rocky countered, glad to have changed the subject away from her performance in the classroom to something she could be angry about. "It's different running alone if you're a girl or a woman. You can't just go. Well, you can. But you always have this thing in your mind. You're wary. It's rubbish. So people say 'run together', but that's not right. It's like there's a curfew for women who are on their own. You can't run alone early in the morning or late in the evening. Why? Because you're a young woman and it's not a good thing to do. What I think… what there needs to be is a curfew for men."

"I get it," Jesse said. "I'm sorry."

Rocky looked at Jesse. "Why?"

"What?"

"Why are you sorry?"

"Because the reason you can't run solo and sort your head out is because of men. And I'm a man."

Rocky shrugged. "I don't suppose it's your fault. Directly."

"Can you run with Kim? Mahsa? Naomi?" Jesse suggested.

"Mahsa and Naomi don't like the hills. They like track, or pitch side. Flat and even. And Kim's not always around…"

Jesse leaned forward, but continued to look out of the window at the hills. "You don't want to run alone, so you don't run. You don't like face-to-face conversations, so you don't talk. How about this? Why don't we run together? Up there. Sometimes in silence. I can even go ahead or drop back. Give you space. Sometimes we talk. What do you think?"

Rocky half liked the sound of that. "Thanks. That would be kind of you."

"But what about you in the classroom?" Jesse smiled. "Can I help with that, too? You know you have a school report coming your way. It has a bearing on things."

"You could go do my classes for me," Rocky said. "Do my homework."

Jesse laughed. "Funny. I'd like to. But, seriously, can I get you help with your homework? We have things in place. Let me help?"

Rocky shrugged. "No. It's my weakness. I should sort it. It's my fault, I mean."

Jesse caught Rocky's eye. "That's not true. It's not your fault. Not your weakness. We just need to find, to focus on, your strengths. I need to think it through. It's about your learning style, maybe?"

"I dunno." Rocky shrugged again. "The only learning style I know is for me to sit in a classroom, stare at a teacher and feel my brain shutting down like the lights being turned off in the school after the end of the day."

Jesse nodded. "So what now?"

"I'll get on top of it," Rocky said. "On my own."

"On your own? You sure you can?"

Rocky was desperate to get away now. Go to see Kim. Go anywhere.

"Yeah," she said, trying hard to convince herself she could change things. "I'm on it."

But she wasn't. Yes, she knew the school report was coming. But she still shut down any thoughts about it that came into her head.

6

TRAINING, ROCKY LIVED for training as the days and weeks passed by.

And, with the sun lower now that it was late October, the pitches were in the shadow of the row of trees that ran alongside the field. That made it easier for Rocky who—much as she liked California sunshine—preferred to train in the shade. Even the dark. She remembered training with Melchester Rovers Women at the sports centre back home, under the floodlights. All-weather pitches. Rain.

Training.

Shuttle runs. Passing drills. Dribbling drills. Then Coach Abby putting them together to work on each other's weaknesses. Abby had encouraged her players to do this. Coach each other. Defenders make the attackers better and vice versa.

Today Rocky was working with Naomi on blocking. Naomi was so great in the air, with her head to the ball first. Awesome at tackling. But it was like she'd never been coached to block.

They played one on one, a goal behind Naomi.

"When I get a chance to shoot," Rocky said, "but I'm in the penalty area, don't tackle me. Work out when I am going to have a go at goal, then drop your arms behind your back and use your legs and upper body to block the ball."

All this was to build up for the first

scrimmage of the season. The first test for them as a team.

Rocky loved it. She was shattered by the end and had been so focused on training that she'd not seen the boys' team waiting pitch side for their session. The soccer girls trained up to half-seven then handed over to the soccer boys who were always keen to get on the pitch, but had been told not to encroach until the girls were off it.

"We're good for the game," Rocky said to Mahsa, as they stretched out to bring training to a close. "Two days and we play Everflowing Fountain."

Mahsa was about to reply when they noticed the boys moving, en masse, onto the pitch while the girls were still cooling down, their ball rolling towards Rocky's feet.

"Get off the field, girls," a boy Rocky didn't know called out. "Time for some real soccer!"

Rocky stopped, blocking their way, flicking their ball up and catching it, about to challenge them. But Mahsa surprised Rocky by edging in front of her.

"Meaning?" Mahsa asked the boy.

Rocky noticed the boy—dark hair, tall, so muscular she assumed he used supplements or worse—had a touch of rage in his eyes.

"Meaning this field has always been the boys' field—since my father and grandfather came here—and you should be grateful we let girls use it."

Mahsa smiled. Rocky kept her mouth shut. As did the rest of her teammates, who had lined up behind their friend like the boys had lined up behind the boy.

"I'm from Iran," Mahsa said.

"Welcome to my country," the boy replied insincerely.

"Thank you," Mahsa said, then she paused

and the whole sports facility seemed to go quiet. Even the wind dropped. "I like your country," Mahsa went on.

"I like my country, too," the boy grinned. "The land of the free."

Mahsa stepped forward, adjusting her headscarf. "If it's called the land of the free, why are you trying to stop women playing?"

The boy smiled. "No offence, but you girls do need to make way for us."

"Meaning what? I don't understand."

"Girls."

"Girls have to make way? Why?"

"Because men's sports trump girls' sports."

"Trump?"

"Yeah."

"Clever choice of words," Mahsa scowled, "for people like you."

Mahsa paused as some of the other girls laughed, appreciating her joke. "Have you heard of Brandi Chastain?" she asked. "Megan Rapinoe? Abby Wambach?"

"Sure. Girl soccer players, won the World Cup. Americans."

"Well, I've not heard of any male US footballers. Have you?"

"Sure I have."

"Name one."

"David Beckham."

"He's British."

The boy shrugged defensively. His friends were laughing at him behind his back now, just like Cody's friends had earlier.

Rocky kept a straight face.

"Do you like Kim Kardashian?" Mahsa asked the boy.

The boy looked like he knew he was in trouble now. His face was pink. His eyes were flitting from side to side. "Yeah. She's... you know... okay?"

"Here's some football news for you. Did you know she funded a girl team's flights out of Afghanistan and that she did it so that they could escape from the Taliban? And that, if they had not escaped, something terrible might have happened? You read things in the news about girls and young women in some countries, in lots of countries. But now—thanks to Kim Kardashian and an English team called Leeds United—they play football in the UK."

"Great," the boy said, looking half cheery, half embarrassed.

Mahsa went on. "So, I come from Iran and play soccer in the US, and Rocky here, she is from the UK and plays in the US. Naomi over there is from Ghana. We can be footballers. But girls in Afghanistan do not always have that privilege. So, I'll thank you for not interrupting us when it is still our time to play."

Rocky now heard a couple more of the other boys laughing at their friend. But most were silent. Waiting for the conversation to end. Uneasy.

Mahsa sensed that too and walked through the boys, parting them, towards the changing rooms, Rocky and her teammates following with pride behind her.

And Rocky could not stop grinning. Mahsa was badass.

THAT NIGHT THEY had another movie night, as planned. Rocky was a bit disappointed that Kim didn't join in. She seemed a bit low. Or quiet. And, when the movie was ten minutes in, she stood up and said she needed an early night.

Although she missed her friend, Rocky didn't worry too much about it. But, an hour and a bit later, going to bed, she noticed Kim's light was on and heard the soft tone of her friend's voice coming though her bedroom wall.

7

THE FIRST GAME Rocky played for Mountain Heights as a full student of the school was in mid-October. And it was against Everflowing Fountain, a team Rocky had been sent off against during the summer camp.

The Everflowing fans, sitting on the three layers of bleachers pitch side, remembered Rocky and booed every time she got the ball.

Rocky loved it. She had no problem being disliked on the football field. This only helped the feeling that she was doing something right. That she was definitely a better player having spent just a few weeks with Abby.

Rocky had never worked under a coach like Abby. Here was a footballer who had played for her country, who had won the World Cup.

"You're better than anyone else on that pitch," Coach Abby had said in a one-to-one the day before. "But you need to stay on it. Stop being so volatile. Keep it tight for the first three quarters. Play deep. Block. Pass your way out. Only tackle when you have to. Then—when the opposition are tired in the last quarter—hit them. But be patient. Don't let them get to you."

Before coming to this school, Rocky had never enjoyed being told where she was going wrong, never restrained herself, controlled herself. She had just played her natural game all the time.

But, for Coach Abby, she was willing to learn.

Rocky did what Abby asked of her.

Controlled the midfield. Sat back. Dealt with the flourishes the opposition had to throw at her. Even when the fans of the opposition booed her, she still sat deep, kept control, didn't tackle hard. Discipline. She repeated the word in her head.

Discipline. Discipline. Discipline.

Abby's words lived within Rocky. Like they'd been downloaded into her head.

Fitness. Patience. Discipline.

Fifteen minutes to go, one goal each, and what Abby had predicted came true. The Everflowing Fountain players weren't reaching their teammates' passes. They didn't have the legs. The ball was going back. Some of the passes were underdone, the ball bouncing loose in centre midfield, where Rocky was.

Now she could push forward, run with the ball. Those were Abby's instructions: push on when Everflowing Fountain are tiring. You'll only stretch them. You have the fitness to track back if you lose it.

If you lose it.

Rocky was nervous the first time. What if I do lose it? What if I leave the defence exposed?

You'll have the pace and the power to get back, Abby had told her. Stretch the game.

Rocky took the ball and ran diagonally right to left, seeing Kim switch left to right. A tackle came in, studs up, but Rocky rode it, took two more touches, then played the ball behind the opposition defence. And there was Kim. One touch for her, drawing the keeper, a shot and a goal.

2–1.

Rocky heard Abby shout out in delight, "Yes! That's it!"

Kim ran alongside Rocky as they returned

for the restart. Then two more teammates—Kenzie and Beth.

"Let's just keep hitting them on the break. Look at them. They're wrecked."

Rocky looked. The Everflowing players who had tried to break up their attack were leaning over, hands on knees.

Rocky heard more boos from the sidelines.

"Again," they heard Abby call. "Go again."

And that's just what they did. Played deep, a solid line.

Naomi blocked a short pass, causing the ball to spin to Mahsa, who tapped it to Rocky in open space. Fast passes. Fast thinking. Rocky looked up to see Beth and Rachel, Kim and Kenzie streaming forward, the opposition completely out of shape. The counterattack was on.

Rocky ran with the ball, fast into the centre circle, two defenders backing off, not tackling. Rocky had a choice of three teammates to pass to.

"Tackle Race!" someone shouted.

Rocky almost laughed. They knew her name. How do they know my name? Rocky wondered, then slid the ball wide and watched as Beth took two touches and ran at an angle into the penalty area, drawing the last defender, then playing across the face of the goal, out of the reach of the keeper.

And there was Kim. Again. Slotting it home.

Rocky knew at 3–1 the game was won. The Everflowing players weren't looking at each other. Their coach had stopped barking instructions.

Rocky jogged over to congratulate Kim on her goal and heard Kenzie say, "You do realise this team made it to the USA national semis last year?"

"Yeah?" Rocky asked, surprised.

"And they're the favourites for the California state championship this year, too," Rachel added.

When Rocky would look back she would identify this as the moment she realised they had a chance. A chance of doing something Mountain Heights—neither the girls' nor the boys' teams—had ever done before. The fact they had won the summer tournament during camp had been amazing. But this? This was the real thing. The state championship. Could they?

8

THE NEXT FIVE games that Mountain Heights played went just as well. In fact, better. Much better.

Rocky had never felt like this about her football before. With every game she was improving. But not just improving, evolving too. Abby was coaching her to not just break the play up, to be destructive. But to be creative. To attack. It was alien to Rocky. And she wondered if that was why she loved it so much. She was flying.

Happy.

Was she really happy?

Yes, she was.

Until her first school report dropped in an email.

It was not great reading, but Rocky was used to that in the UK. She had never excelled at school. It was the comment from Abby—not from the teachers like Mrs Achebe—that hurt.

Abby, who had been building her and boosting her all term. Challenging her. Praising her. Celebrating her, even. And now this.

You need to improve your grades significantly. If not, even if we make the national finals, you won't be on the team.

Rocky slammed her laptop shut and stared at the hills. Her head was throbbing. She needed to get out. Now. Get out of her room, their flat and the grounds of the school and away from everyone.

Grades were her Achilles' Heel. The football and her new friendships and freedom would count for nothing if she didn't get the grades.

For a moment, Rocky wished her brother was here so she could have a go at him, wind him up, create a row. That was how she used to get things off her chest back home. But Roy wasn't here and that sort of game didn't play out so well screen to screen.

Run. Alone. Rocky would run. That was the answer. There were still a few hours of daylight left.

Changed and outside the school gates, she started to run north-east, heading for the hills. After three, four, five strides, she slowed to a stop. The hills. She stared at them. She couldn't run in the hills. How many people had told her not to go up in the hills on her own?

But she needed to run alone. Rocky hung

her head and closed her eyes, then cursed the stupid man who had done what he'd done and the world for being so rubbish that a woman or a girl couldn't go for a run on her own in the hills.

The sun was easing down in the west. It would dip below the horizon soon. As if it was sinking into the sea.

The sea, yes. The sea was where she'd go! To the beach. Not a bad second option, although she still resented not having the choice to do what she wanted.

Rocky turned and began to run stop-start through built-up streets, waiting for the walk sign to cross roads. She could taste the petrol fumes in the air, but she still pushed on. She'd be at the coast soon. It was only a ten-minute run.

Rocky made a choice to run through the hospital car park with its palm trees and watered lawns. To avoid the traffic. The hospital grounds were almost like a city park. A shortcut to the beach. Rocky realised that this was a route that took you off the streets and mostly on grass right to the beach. And the air was better. Breathable.

Result.

And then—as she ran—a parked car caught her eye. Located near a sign saying ONCOLOGY. The car was white, large and had a silhouette image of a footballer stickered on the back window. She knew that car.

Kim's mum's car. Rocky knew it was hers. She'd seen it when Kim's mum had dropped her off at school more than once. What was she doing here?

It must be work, Rocky thought.

Forgetting Kim's mum, Rocky jogged on, out of the hospital grounds. Underneath the eight-lane highway that cut between the taller buildings and the area before the beach, where there were bars and small shops and then, stretching out towards the sparkling waves and sky, the beach itself.

Legs warmed up now and with no cars to worry about, Rocky ran the last half mile onto the beach at seventy-five per cent speed. Easy to keep up for one or two minutes, not for five minutes. But she pushed herself. Ever since Abby had praised her fitness, Rocky had only wanted to be fitter. As fit as the US teammates Abby used to play alongside.

Breathless and laughing, Rocky staggered to a halt and stood with her running shoes almost in the Pacific Ocean. She loved what she could make her body do, how strong she could make herself feel. How fit.

As long as she was doing that she didn't think about how she did not have the same control of her brain or her thoughts. And then she remembered what Coach Abby had said in her comments on her report card.

Even if we make the national finals, you won't be on the team.

Was that true? And, if so, was all this footballing progress, this fitness, pointless?

"And what if I can't do it?" she said to the sea as the sun dipped below the horizon and the clouds and vapour trails of planes heading away from California illuminated orange, then faded to grey as colour drained from the beach and the sea and—finally— the sky.

It doesn't matter if I'm the best player on the team. If I mess up in the classroom, I'm on one of those planes out of here.

9

AFTER TWENTY-FOUR HOURS of school report angst, Rocky was back on the football field.

And she was angry.

She'd had a bad night's sleep. At first, it had been about her grades and Abby's remark. But then—later—she'd become upset as she thought more and more about seeing Kim's mum's car outside the hospital. And not just any part of the hospital, but the oncology department. Was this something to do with why Kim was not herself? Was there something terrible going on in her best friend's life and she had no idea about it?

And—then—outside at three a.m. she'd seen a group of older students carrying a coffin through the school grounds, laughing their heads off. She knew what this was, of course. Halloween. The whole school had been decked out in skulls and ghosts and tombstones. Cobwebs and glowing green evil eyes hung from every doorway.

The annual celebration of death.

This only made Rocky angrier. Halloween was fun. She'd gone trick or treating until she was ten. Then it all turned a bit nasty and people would just do destructive things at home and school. Play practical jokes. And think it was okay to do damage to people and property because it was Halloween. Rocky had always hated practical jokes. The worst bit was you were meant to laugh even when you'd been upset. Even after your dad was dead and you were half worried his ghost would be among the damned and the doomed that were supposed to be such fun every October.

Rocky had come to hate Halloween.

And now? Even more so.

Suddenly, after a cheery start, there were so many things that felt like they were getting in the way of a happy life in California. School work. Halloween. Seeing Kim's mum's car outside ONCOLOGY. That was the killer. Literally.

Because Rocky knew what oncology meant.

It meant cancer.

As she lay there stressing that Kim's mum might have cancer and how bad that would make Kim feel, it brought all her own memories back about her dad and his cancer. All those feelings she had gone through were here again, as raw as they were when Dad was diagnosed, suffered his illness, then died. It was horrible.

The bad night was followed by a worse day in school, with Rocky not going to her last class. Just not going. Which she would have to explain later.

So it was a relief, the next day, to be back on a football field, playing football.

The match was against Ocean View, a school from up the coast who had come to defend deep and not concede. Alert to this, Rocky was trying to do what Abby had praised her for, encouraged her to do: win the ball in the middle of the field. Control it. Look up for options. Then—late in the game—run with the ball. Attack.

Rocky made that choice with just fifteen minutes to go, like in the game before. Most players were tiring, and she was not. Also like in the game before. Fitness made such a difference. She'd go fast forward and see if she could break the defence that way.

One touch, two touches, Rocky shouldered her way through a tackle, allowing the ball to run on ahead of her, relying on her pace to get her into a dangerous position. And then—from nowhere—an Ocean View player slide tackled her, skimming across the grass, taking the ball, then righting herself in one slick movement, to begin a counterattack.

It was fair. It was highly skillful. And Rocky was furious.

Furious, because it had been at her expense. She had been undone, outplayed. And now all the confusion and angst of the last twenty-four hours exploded inside her, and she ploughed after her tackler.

She ran fast. She ran hard. There was no way this girl was going to get away with taking the ball from her. Catching up with her tackler, Rocky scythed her to the ground, not bothering to take the ball.

The player cried out, the ball ran free, and three of the Ocean View players came over to push at Rocky.

"What was that?" said one of them.

"A foul," Rocky muttered.

"What are you trying to do?"

"Foul her," Rocky said more loudly. Because she felt wonderfully calm now she'd booted this girl hard. "Isn't it obvious?"

Now Rocky saw a yellow card thrust in her face. She nodded, glad it wasn't red, as she had unfinished business with the player still writhing on the ground.

Seriously, she'd only clipped her. Why was she still whining? Rocky stood hands on hips, feet placed apart, staring at her.

Then an arm around her. Kim's arm.

Rocky felt a weakness run through her limbs. Like Kim's touch had disarmed her.

Kim glanced towards the sideline. "She's

bringing you off," Kim said in a low voice, her arm still around Rocky.

"Who is? What?"

"Abby. She's subbing you. Come on."

Kim was pulling at Rocky, wanting to get her away from the point of conflict.

If it had been anyone else, Rocky would have slipped free. Even pushed them away. But it was Kim, and Kim had lots to cope with. So Rocky went willingly with her friend.

The game continued. Without Rocky.

Rocky had been benched. Now all she could do was watch. She shrugged and sat down, accepting a bottle of water from Jesse, who raised an eyebrow and smiled.

"Shall we?" Abby asked, leaning into Rocky.

"What?" Rocky still had fight or flight adrenaline in her veins. "Dance?"

"Talk," Abby countered. Her voice was deep. Serious. "Come on."

Jesse took over the touchline, as Abby walked Rocky away from the action.

"Problem?"

"Me?"

"Yeah, you. You're channelling your old ways. What's going on?"

Rocky realised that Abby was spot on. She was behaving, reacting and thinking like the old Rocky. She considered making up something to pretend she thought otherwise. But no. She didn't do that any more. She'd shoot from the hip. People liked her to be direct. Just spill it all. Especially to Abby.

"I read what you put in my report," Rocky said. "It panicked me. I saw Kim's mum's car outside the cancer ward: it reminded me of my dad dying and I don't want Kim to have to go through that. I like Kim."

"And you need to bring all that onto the pitch?" Abby asked, still looking cross.

"Yeah. Normally I do. That's why I play football. But that girl… she's been diving all game. It's the first time I actually fouled her."

Abby shook her head. "I don't want that. I want you to play because you're good. Not because you're angry. You need to leave it all in the locker room. You're my soccer player now. Not some angry British football kid out to break legs. I'm trying to coach you to be the best. Not… that. And, anyway, that girl tackled you beautifully. I would have her on my team any day."

Rocky winced. Abby was disapproving of her. Abby was praising someone else, not her. She heard that loud and clear. And it hurt.

"Well," Rocky said, knowing she shouldn't go on, knowing she was being like she used to be, all anger and self-destruction, but not being able to stop the words erupting from that anger. "There's no point in helping me with football if you can't help me excel in those stupid classrooms too, because then I'm going home, aren't I?"

10

LATER THAT EVENING, Rocky and Kim sat together in the living room they shared with Mahsa and Naomi. It was the only room in their suite that was impersonal. In their rooms, they had posters and blankets from home that made their spaces their own. Even the bathroom was cluttered with towels and bathrobes and make-up bags that made the room seem like a home. Their sitting room could have been anyone's room.

As usual, the other two girls were in the library. Rocky hadn't been in the library since being given a tour of the school on day one.

She didn't do libraries.

"So what was that about?" Kim asked. "That foul."

Rocky looked at her friend and shrugged, drawing a smile. She had wanted to ask her friend why she hadn't decorated the flat with Halloween stuff like the rest of the school. But decided not to. Halloween was about death. Maybe Kim was not into that this year. Maybe she had a good reason?

The question about the foul was a fair question. Rocky accepted that. What had her sudden reverse into brutal football been to do with? Was it about her grades? Or was it about Kim's mum and the whole cancer thing? That image of her mum's car and the word ONCOLOGY kept coming back to Rocky. Like a dream she was having over and over again, but while awake. It could be that. Rocky felt rubbish about it. She had this thing she maybe knew about her best friend. Maybe the best friend she'd ever had. But she hadn't told her.

"I don't know," Rocky said, then stood up. "I think I need to call Mum."

Kim looked uneasy, like she wanted to talk to Rocky really, rather than the other way round. But Rocky felt awkward, so she turned.

"Do you want to talk?" Rocky asked.

"Me? No. What about?"

"I dunno. It's fine. See you in a bit, yeah?"

Alone in her bedroom, Rocky pulled the blinds shut and dialled home.

"Hey, Mum."

"Hey, love." Mum sounded sleepy.

"Oh no!" Rocky hadn't thought about the time difference. "I'm sorry, what time is it?"

"It doesn't matter. I'd wake up at three in the morning for a chat with you."

"Yeah, but what time is it?" Rocky insisted.

"Three in the morning," Mum laughed.

"Sorry."

"It's no biggie," Mum said. Rocky could tell that she was smiling from the sound of her voice. "Talk to me."

"I need to ask you something," Rocky said. "Just quickly."

"Okay."

"So… I saw Kim's mum's car outside the local cancer ward today. Kim says she's been a bit funny recently. But I don't know if she knows anything about her mum going there. And I love Kim and feel like I am keeping something from her." Rocky took a breath. "So what do I do?"

Mum didn't answer straight away. And Rocky knew to wait because Mum was thinking, and liked space and time to do so.

Rocky stared at a photo she had of her

mum on the wall. Just a little one from one of those instant cameras she'd had when she was a child. She'd found the camera again while packing to come to the US and taken a photo of her mum for her wall here. She saw her mum's gaze, a gentle smile. She'd taken the photo the day before she headed off to California.

"And are you okay?" Mum asked.

"I don't care about me," Rocky shot back. "This is about Kim."

"And it is about you too, honey," Mum pressed. "These are your feelings about you, too. I can hear it in your voice."

Rocky shook her head. She didn't want to talk about her feelings. This was about Kim and Kim's mum. Rocky was impatient.

"Do I tell her?" she insisted.

"Is it for you to tell?" Mum asked. "I mean, isn't it up to her mum?"

Rocky snapped. "Her mum is being cruel. Doesn't she have a right to know if her mum is really ill?"

"She might not be really ill. She might just be having tests. She might even be visiting a friend. It could be anything."

"So I just tell her I saw the car? I'm not saying to her that her mum's got cancer and am keeping it from her, am I?"

"I see what you mean. But…"

"But what? I really like Kim. I've never had a friend like her and we're so open about everything, we… And her mum is so nice. I hate to think of her going through what we… What Dad…"

"Love, you're upset."

"Forget me. Of course I am upset. But I need to know what to do."

Rocky took three deep breaths. She was feeling panic again. She hated panic. First her body felt out of control, then her thoughts. It was unbearable to be inside herself.

"It's her mum's business," Mum said again.

Rocky didn't reply.

"But listen, love," Mum went on, "what you do is up to you. I am not telling you what to do. I'm just saying what I would do."

Rocky felt a spasm in her throat. She put her hands to her eyes and felt wetness.

"I'm crying," she told her mum.

"That's okay," Mum assured her. "I'm here."

They shared a silence where Rocky couldn't speak and her mum didn't.

"It brought it all back," Rocky told her mum.

"I understand," Mum said softly. "Listen… with that in mind, think about… if you can, if it helps… think about what you would have felt like if someone had told you about your dad being ill before we told you. Or if they'd not told you. How would you have felt?"

Rocky wanted to tell her mum how she was feeling in her head, but she couldn't, could she? How would Mum feel if she knew that she was panicky again? Mum would be unable to do anything so many thousands of miles away.

Best to calm herself down. Best not to upset her mum. Best to bury the panic and the worry and make Mum assume she was okay. Best for Mum.

"You're right," Rocky said, hoping to sound calm. "I'll leave it. You're right, Mum. Thanks. I feel so much better now."

11

GAME FOLLOWED GAME quickly, now the soccer season had begun in earnest.

This one was a serious game, too. A meaningful game.

This was the pre-qualifier they were expected to breeze through. One of those games you just have to turn up to and win. To show respect to the opposition, yes. But to know, deep down, that it's a win. Every time.

The opposition were a school from an inland and rural part of California—called Hooverville—that had had some success with American football, but never in soccer. They were there because they had just introduced a girls' soccer programme and for that reason only.

And the home side, Mountain Heights, had a structure now. A solid defence held together by the axis of Mahsa and Naomi. A playbreaker and playmaker just in front of them in Rocky. And Kim and Kenzie and Beth free running ahead of her. With seven wins from seven that season, qualification for Mountain Heights was a given. The script read a clear win for Mountain Heights, a one-way ticket to the California state championship qualifiers.

But Hooverville had not read the script.

Ten minutes into the game—with Mountain Heights probing deeper and deeper into Hooverville's territory—the visitors' tall lean forward came deep, frustrated at not having had a touch of the ball yet. Intercepting a pass Rocky played up for Kim to run on to, the visitor won possession. Then, with the ball at her feet, she ran the length of the pitch, riding tackles, finding space to run and run with such pace that by the time she was in on goal she was on her own. Just Ella to beat. Which she did.

Mountain Heights 0, Hooverville 1.

It had happened so fast that no one believed it. Like watching a goal on YouTube that you've seen a hundred times and you know just what the defending team should have done to stop it, but they never did, however many times you watched it.

Kim and Rocky reacted to the goal by running alongside their teammates as they took up positions for the restart.

"We've got this," Kim said. "We play our way for ninety minutes. With possession, we play it fast and short out from the back.

Without possession we harry them until they make errors. Come on."

Kim was saying just what Coach Abby drilled into them each week. It was their philosophy. It was what they trained for. They'd even trained for this scenario exactly. How would they react if they conceded an early goal? How would they recover and not be too stunned to do so?

By doing what Coach Abby had drilled into them. That's what they needed to do. To be. Play the Mountain Heights way. Stick to the principles.

But—for whatever reason—the Mountain Heights game did not play out. For Rocky in particular, she struggled to find Kim. Kim wasn't in the right place to take the pass. And without that channel for their team to attack, there was no other way they could dominate the game. At the back, the defence were playing deeper, far more cautious than usual, like the pace of the Hooverville striker and her goal had got into their heads. And even though they all knew what was happening, they couldn't seem to change it.

Each time Rocky won the ball, she would look at her options: a back pass, play it wide to Rebecca on the left, or Lexi on the right. Thread a pass up field to Beth or Kim. Or run with it. Options they had trained for over and over. With the Kim option being the number one option.

But today that option didn't come off once. Kim was never in the right place. Kim wasn't calling for it. Or Rocky didn't have quite the right control of the ball to naturally play it to her friend.

And then there was her aggression. The engine that drove Rocky's entire game. Rocky had nothing.

"What's up with you?" Kim asked Rocky as they wandered off the pitch at half time, still one goal down.

Rocky knew she wasn't right. Normally she was able to walk onto a football pitch and forget everything. Absolutely everything. She would leave her troubles on the sideline and not give them a thought. Even when her dad was dying, then dead. She knew she was failing to do that today.

"I was going to ask you the same thing," Rocky said, meaning it as a joke.

Then, one of those uncomfortable glances you exchange with a normally close friend when you're not quite on the same page. Or pitch. Or field.

Rocky looked away first. She had an image of Kim's mum at the oncology ward, then of her dad all tubed up when he was really ill. Why were those images coming into her head on the football pitch? All her life, she had been able to leave everything and anything off the pitch. But not today.

Without saying anything else to each other, Rocky and Kim joined their teammates in a tight circle pitch side. Abby entered the circle. None of them were talking.

"So," Abby said. "Our whole season will be determined by the next forty-five minutes. And we need a quick fix."

The girls all eyed each other. They knew what 'quick fix' meant: one or two players were going to be substituted. In the two or three seconds Abby took to size up her players, Rocky wondered who it would be. One of the wide midfielders, Kenzie or Rebecca? Maybe they'd not been sharp enough to offer an outlet for Rocky. Or Beth, upfront with Kim? Abby had form for replacing a forward with a new skillset. It was just like using a different tool to open a can. Find a goal.

Or Kim? Maybe Kim? She seemed off her game. Rocky waited, heard Abby speak, but missed it, she was so caught up in her thoughts.

It was then that she noticed everyone was looking at her. Then back at Abby. And it dawned on her. She was the one coming off.

"Me?" she asked Abby.

Abby nodded. "You're miles off your game. I think you're getting sick with something. Your passes are off. And your aggression. We all have days like this. I'm pulling you off, Rocky."

12

ROCKY'S INITIAL REACTION to being substituted was rage.

You've been dropped from the team in what has become an all-or-nothing qualifier. You had started to think of yourself as a key player. You could just go off, be cross. Why not?

And who the hell was Abby to drop her? What did she know?

Rocky closed her eyes and felt a heat like a firework going off in her head. Red mist. Fury. Anger. Rage. She squatted on the edge of the pitch and screwed up her face, pretended to do her laces, so she could get a grip.

Who was Abby? Abby was her coach. The boss. A former US international.

What did she know? She knew everything.

Think, Rocky said to herself, trying to cool her head off. Don't react. She'll know you're angry. Let her see that, then let her see you do the right thing. You can do this. You can be in control with football, even if you're not with school work.

Rocky was replaced in central midfield by Kim, and Lexi was sent on to play wide in Kim's place.

Deep breath. Deep breath. Slow. Calm. Steady.

Rocky felt better. A bit better. If she couldn't help on the pitch, she'd help off it.

"Come on," Rocky shouted from the touchline, clapping her hands each time a Hooverville attack broke down and the momentum shifted to Mountain Heights.

It took only five minutes for Kim to make the most of her new deep position. Moving forward with the ball, she drew three Hooverville players, then fired a ball out wide to Lexi, the substitute. Next she ran fast up field, arm raised, demanding the ball.

It was a simple move. Aggressive. Easy to defend if you'd worked on it on the training field. But Hooverville hadn't, and now they looked out of their depth.

Rocky punched the air when Kim scored, receiving a pass back from Lexi, two touches, drawing the keeper, then clipping it past her. Rocky watched Kim and Lexi celebrate with a hug and felt a pang of jealousy, but pushed it away. She wanted Kim to be happy, even if it wasn't with her. Especially with what might be going on with her mum.

And then those thoughts again. Dead parent thoughts. Why couldn't she shake them off?

She didn't want these thoughts, but here they were. Again.

Rocky was pretty sure that Kim didn't know about her mum. Gazing off to the mountains, she remembered being told her dad was ill and understanding straight away that she'd seen signs for months. Like she'd known in her subconscious. The signs had been there to see. Like Dad being clumsy. Like Mum being different, more loving, her parents not arguing any more, even over little things. Like routine hospital appointments that weren't routine at all, but Rocky didn't question them. As soon as Mum told her Dad was ill it was as if she'd known for weeks.

Rocky had not put two and two together. But then she'd never been good at maths.

Rocky was gazing at the mountains when she heard cheers. She looked back at the pitch to see Kim celebrating again.

2–1.

They were winning now. Abby's substitution had worked. Dropping Rocky had worked. Rocky raised her hands above her head and clapped for the team.

Smiling and sitting on the grass behind Ella's goal, Rocky studied her friends and the school. She closed her eyes and again her thoughts flitted between now and the football, home and Mum.

Rocky wondered what her mum would be doing now. It was eleven in the morning in California. So about seven p.m. at home. Mum would be drawing the curtains to keep the cold out. It'd be dark by seven now in England. It would probably be raining. Inside the front room Mum would be eating something she'd made. Alone. Probably soup. She loved to make her own soup. And Roy would be in London. He had an away game there. Rocky wondered if Mum would eat in front of the TV or in the kitchen. And if she was in the kitchen, would she be looking at the three empty chairs at the table? How would that make her feel? Her eighteen-year-old son was away from home to be a footballer. Her husband was dead. And her fourteen-year-old daughter was thousands of miles away.

Then a sob. It came from nowhere like a sneeze or a cough. But it was a sob. And a sob was different. What was happening to her? She pushed her feelings down. She shut her thoughts off.

Another whoop as Kim ran to Lexi to celebrate a third goal. 3–1. Mountain Heights were through to the California state championship qualifiers.

Rocky winced, then clapped again, forcing a smile, feigning enthusiasm, knowing people would be looking at her to see how she felt about being replaced and things being much improved for it.

Was her team winning without her a sign? she wondered.

A sign that she wasn't good enough on the pitch and that, anyway, her grades really were not good enough. Did it mean that she was wrong to think she was happy in the US, that she had a future in football, that she actually wasn't happy and that she really belonged back home in Melchester?

And how did all this relate to Kim's mum and her own dad? And did any of it matter, because the bottom line was that if she couldn't improve her grades—even if she was good at football—she was going home anyway?

It was horribly confusing.

Maybe she shouldn't be here.

13

WITH THE COMING of Thanksgiving and following qualification for the state championship, the competitive football fixtures had finished.

Being British, Rocky had never really deep down understood what Thanksgiving was. She'd seen it in countless American films. It was a time for family celebration. Turkey. Pumpkins. That sort of thing. She was never sure if it was Christmas or if it was Halloween. Now—as her teammates went off to celebrate with their parents and grandparents—she got it. It was Harvest Festival.

The team celebrated with a turkey dinner outside by the football fields. There was a speech and then—in a surprise move—Abby stood up and announced she would be away from the beginning of December to the end of February. She had another job to do, although she said nothing about what it was.

The holiday mood evaporated.

Jesse was asked to keep the girls going until the Christmas break with three ninety-minute training sessions a week. Two in the evenings, under floodlights. One on Saturday morning. Drills. Fitness. More drills. Strength. Fitness. And going over and over plays that had worked for them in competitive games.

That pattern went on from late November and into December. Deep down, Rocky resented that Abby had gone. Abby was the reason Rocky had come here. To learn from her. To become a better player. To live a dream that included great football coaching. She had not even worked it out herself, but Rocky was cross with Abby and cross with the school.

Even so, Rocky's football was fine. She felt she was training well, though uncertain how she'd play in a proper game next time after the Hooverville tie when she'd been subbed. You could never really tell, never replicate the intensity of a competitive match. She was not sure how she would play in the next game. Then again, she was not sure if she would. The whole thing with Kim and her mum and thoughts about Rocky's dad and mum had thrown her. She wanted to characterise it as homesickness but wasn't sure about that.

The bottom line was Rocky felt like she was playing well. And she knew she was a good footballer. This was no crisis of confidence. Just frustration she had not proved herself yet.

But she would.

The rest of their lives was classroom. Inside four walls. Sat at a desk. A teacher at the front. A smart board. The backs of people's heads to stare at. An awareness that there were people staring at the back of your head. Feeling like a misshaped cog in a machine.

All the football girls seemed perfectly happy in the classroom. Rocky was only happy outside it. When the school bell rang for break her heart lifted in her chest and she longed to be out in the corridor, standing at the lockers chatting. At least she sat next to Kim at lunch. That made her happy. Just being near her friend was enough some days.

But on the first day of the last week before everyone travelled home for Christmas, Kim was not there. Rocky assumed she needed to be at home with her mum. Nor was Mahsa, who had returned to Iran, taking the chance to go home and spend some time with her family. Rocky knew about Mahsa. But Rocky did wonder where Kim was. She'd just not been there that morning and had not replied to Rocky's text.

Naomi took the opportunity to sit with Rocky and, in the break, they walked to go outside in the pale sunshine. Rocky lifted her face to the warmth. She'd miss the California winter.

"Rocky? Can I ask you something?"

"Sure." Rocky turned to look at Naomi. She had been about to ask Naomi if she was going home to Ghana for the holiday. But there was a seriousness in Naomi's voice. Like she had something important to ask Rocky, to tell her. Perhaps Naomi was thinking of leaving, too?

"It is about you in the classroom," Naomi stuttered. "I don't want to be rude. But I can't understand something. Tell me not to pry…"

"It's fine, Naomi. We're friends. You can say anything, Just ask."

Naomi swallowed. Then she started: "I don't understand why you don't put your hand up, talk in class. You are a great talker. And I don't understand why, when we are supposed to write, you stare out of the window. Or close your eyes. Why?"

Rocky took in a deep breath. It was a good question. Annoying from most people, but not Naomi, Naomi so clearly wanted to understand what she could not. She was not being rude.

"I can't concentrate," she explained. "It's boring. My mind just goes off in another direction when someone is talking to me. I want to press fast forward. I can't bear it."

"Bear what?"

"Being in the classroom. School. Lessons. Teachers."

A silence. Naomi doesn't get me, Rocky thought.

"So why are you here?" Naomi pressed. "It's a school."

"For the football. Like you. We both got scholarships to be footballers here."

Naomi shook her head. "No. I am here for the school. The football is a happy addition."

"Oh right… yeah. I get it."

"But you… I don't understand how you are a girl from England and you are at this amazing American school. You can learn. It's a chance you have to take."

Rocky smiled. "Schools are good in England. Just as good as this."

"Really?"

"'Course."

"So why did your English schools not teach you well?"

Rocky had to laugh before answering. She

loved Naomi's directness: she would fit in well in the north of England.

"It was me. Not the schools. I just hate school. It's horrible. In England. Here. It's just painful."

"But you are the cleverest, funniest, best talker I know. You are so clever."

"I can talk, yes. I can make a joke, yes. But I can't sit in a room listening to an adult telling me stuff that I have to write down and remember. I'd rather stare out of the window, go on my phone. When I'm there... in the classroom... I'd rather be anywhere else."

"But if you fail in the classroom, you have to go home and can't come back."

There she was again. Naomi—the teller of truths—cutting to the chase. Rocky said nothing.

"I'll help you," Naomi said suddenly. "You've helped me so much with training.

You taught me how to block. Now I can repay you?"

Rocky smiled at her friend. It was a kind idea. A lovely idea. But would it mean anything if Rocky decided she was not coming back anyway?

14

Rocky had made the decision to leave Mountain Heights at 3:12 that morning. She had woken up suddenly with a massive pressure on her chest, just like she used to have at home. Like the world was pressing down on her and she couldn't breathe and was going to die if she didn't do something, change something. But what could you do when the world was trying to crush you?

Change.

And this panic—because that's what it was—wasn't just about her grades and the need she felt to do better in the classroom: it was about Kim's mum and what that meant for Kim, and also about what all that meant to her. And the fact that Kim was sometimes not at school and that Rocky wondered if it was to do with her mum being ill, but that they had not spoken about it and how weird it was that they hadn't. And that look they had shared in the last game when they didn't connect. That all of this—every single thing on its own—was too much.

The panic was physical. Like someone had placed her suitcase, packed by the side of her bed, on her chest and was using it to push her down into the mattress. That feeling she'd lived with for months after her dad was ill and had died… it was coming back. It was unbearable. And it made Rocky want to escape. Escape California. Escape football. Escape Kim, even.

After weeks of being terrified of being

kicked out of school and surviving, just, she was now about to choose to leave? Really?

A FEW HOURS later, Rocky was in the school minibus taking her to the airport. Kim sat next to her. Said she needed to see her off and had only come back to school for that reason. Rocky was thrilled Kim wanted to take that last chance to see her. It gave her an opportunity to tell her.

"I'm thinking I might not come back." Rocky said it staring straight ahead, watching trucks and cars and buses battle for space on the fast-moving freeway.

Kim didn't reply for a while.

"Why?" Kim asked eventually, staring back at Rocky. Her voice was almost hostile.

As the minibus approached the airport, the sound of engines reverse thrusting and the smell of aviation fuel invading her senses, Kim took Rocky's hand. No words, not looking at each other, but watching a huge plane drifting over the freeway as if it was as light as a feather and not the heaviest thing.

How do aeroplanes just hang in the sky like that? Rocky heard herself think. How do people carry so many worries in their heads and hearts when they could weigh so much?

Kim interrupted Rocky's thoughts. "You need to talk to me," she said.

Was this the time? Should Rocky tell her? Should she go against what Mum had said and tell Kim what she knew?

Rocky took a deep breath.

No.

It was too much. The weight of the world. The idea that Kim was about to live what she had lived and suffered and hated. And the worse thing was that all Rocky could do was run away, abandon her friend when her friend needed her most. But the pressure on her chest and the chaos of her thoughts were too much. She could hardly speak.

"I can't do school work. I hate it."

"I'll help you."

"I can't be helped."

And now they were both laughing. Rocky wasn't sure why. Then not laughing.

The minibus slowed at a junction and joined a queue of cars going through an underpass, a huge luxury bus behind them, slamming its brakes on. Then on to where passengers could be dropped off to wheel their suitcases under strip lights and over shiny, hard floors. They were at the airport.

Departures.

Rocky thought about her suitcase. It had everything in it. She'd not told Kim or the others, but she'd emptied her room. Posters, photos, ornaments, everything. All in the suitcase. She'd thrown two bin bags of stuff out in the refuse area before anyone else was up. Her room looked like it did the day she arrived. Bare spaces on the walls. Impersonal.

"Abby will be devastated," Kim said. "She told me. She thinks we have a chance of doing well at the national championship, not just the state championship. She wants to build a team around you to do that. She said that."

"I'm sorry," was all Rocky could think to say. She glanced at Kim. "I'll go. See you."

"Will you?"

The question felt to Rocky like she'd been hit by the bus behind them.

Her voice would not work. It was hard not to break down in front of her friend. What could she do? Grab Kim and tell her she was the best friend she'd ever had, then tell her about her mum?

No.

"I don't know," Rocky said.

Kim's eyes widened and her shoulders dropped. "Have a good flight..." she said quietly.

It was too much. Rocky felt like she was going to explode.

Kim put her hand on Rocky's shoulder. "There's something you're not telling me, isn't there? Please tell me there is something else. I can't..."

Rocky felt like her heart really would explode now. She slid her shoulder from under Kim's hand and moved in for a hug. She squeezed her friend tight and her friend squeezed back.

Then Rocky was outside the minibus, saying thank you to Joan the driver and wheeling her suitcase to departures, and away from this life in the US that she had thought was the answer to all her troubles.

15

FOR HOURS AND hours of the flight Rocky stared down at the ice. At Greenland. At Iceland. At half-frozen sea. Rocky loved a window seat and would always book early to secure one. Loved to see the world go by far below. Work out which land mass was which. Maybe see the eerie glowing patterns of the Northern Lights, the reason she had booked a seat on the left-hand side of the plane. And she appreciated that the ice and dark and bleakness matched her mood. Her thoughts were so slow she felt like they were trapped in ice like ships once were in the oceans below.

Aeroplanes that fly from the US to Europe head high above the Arctic Circle and not straight across the Atlantic. Rocky knew that, though she didn't know why.

Rocky was deep inside her thoughts. Thoughts that kept asking her the same question over and over again. Why was this new dream life in the States not making her happy? Why did she feel sad or cross or confused all the time? Was it meant to be like this? And where was she? Where was the old Rocky? Anxious and uneasy, yes. But happy a lot of the time. Excited a lot of the time. Where was she? Had she changed?

Rocky let out a long and exhausted sigh.

On the seats next to her, a young dad and his five-year-old daughter were speculating about whether they'd be able to see the North Pole. The girl was trying to look past Rocky.

Rocky smiled and caught the dad's eyes.

Here was a memory this little girl might keep forever. Of being high above the Arctic and searching for Santa with her dad. The girl might need that memory one day. Who was to say her dad would still be alive when she was fifteen, even ten?

Rocky rolled her eyes at herself. Her dad was everywhere. He'd been dead for less than two years, but he was in every decision, every thought. There was no escaping him. Her mind went back to the girl and her dad next to her and she made a decision.

"I think it's time we swapped seats," she said to the dad. "Then you should be able to see Santa's workshop."

Rocky watched the little girl grab her dad's hand in excitement.

For the rest of the flight, sitting in the aisle seat now, Rocky pretended to be asleep. In her mind she played with the idea that she was in between one life and another. The US and the UK. The past and the future. Mum versus Kim. Family versus friends. Wearing the Mountain Heights school kit against wearing the red and yellow Melchester Rovers strip. All the things that were different. Certainly one life versus another.

Rocky knew she had a decision to make.

But which life would she choose? How could she get back to feeling like she used to, being who she felt she wanted to be? Did she want to be this gloomy? Was it worth it? Where was the real Rocky Race?

16

At first Rocky and her mum were nervous with each other. They hugged a brilliant, almost painful hug together at arrivals. They grinned wildly at each other. Mum cried a little. And Rocky had to fight hard not to. But nervous still. As if they had forgotten how to talk to each other. Did this always happen the first time you'd been away from home for a few weeks? Like they were strangers. Were they strangers? This felt so weird.

There was a message from Kim on Rocky's phone when she took it out of flight mode.

Hope you landed okay.
Hope your mom is good,
too. K.

Rocky replied, pleased that she could say that Mum looked well. And she did. It was true. She was wearing clothes Rocky had not seen before. New clothes? And she had her hair highlighted. But most of all it was in her eyes. There was a sparkle there, and that was good news.

It was cold outside the airport. But deliciously cold. Icy, but warm if you had a coat on. And her mum had brought her one of her two coats.

Rocky breathed in the English winter air and smiled, looking around. She was back. The buildings and the shape of the trees and the advertisements on hoardings and what people were wearing and the colour of the road signs.

It was all so familiar, so different to the US. It was comforting and discomforting at the same time.

"How was the flight?" Mum asked.

Rocky told Mum about the little girl searching for Santa's workshop. Her mum praised her for being kind, but that wasn't why Rocky had told her.

In the car, sleet settling almost snowlike on the windscreen, they asked each other questions. But it was hard to have a joined-up conversation. Neither of them commented on the fact that this was their second Christmas without Dad and that the first Christmas had been so tough that they had barely done any of the things they used to do, like see the Christmas lights in town and go to church for midnight mass. They'd not spoken about it since. They both knew it. They both would be thinking it. Roy would be too. But would any of them say it? Probably not. What was the point?

Rocky's dread that this was going to be a tough couple of weeks surged inside her. She was already thinking she wanted to get away, back to the sunshine and warmth of California. What had she been doing thinking about leaving all that? She felt like she was back in the plane, above the millions of miles of ice and darkness, in that in-between life.

After telling Mum a few more things about Mountain Heights and Mum telling her about home things, Rocky registered that Mum came off the inner ring road early, heading into Melchester city centre, not round it. Maybe there were roadworks? Something like that. It was a different route than normal.

And then—as they approached the centre of town—the sky started to change colour. Just how Rocky had hoped the Northern Lights would look. Greens and reds and sparkling bright whites. They were following a trail of Christmas lights, strung in triangles across the road.

Rocky smiled.

The colours became more intense as they came to the central square. The town hall's windows and doors and the lines of its shape were draped in lights, too. It was magical. And then the tree. A huge Christmas tree in the middle of the square, its lights sparkling all the more through the windscreen.

Mum stopped the car in a bus lane.

"You might get a ticket," Rocky said.

"I don't care," Mum whispered. "I wanted to see this with you. Share it with you. I am thrilled you have this amazing life in the States. But I still want to see the Melchester Christmas lights and the Melchester Christmas tree with you every year, then I can remember it all year."

Rocky smiled. A rush of happiness suffused her. She grabbed her mum's hand and held it. She felt like she was five again, like the little girl on the plane.

How she had hated that American TV phrase about making memories. But here was her mum doing just that, like Rocky had tried to do for that dad and girl on the plane.

Making memories. It might be cheesy, but it was real. It was a nice phrase. She got it now.

"Shall we go home?" Mum asked. "Roy's in bed. And Ffion."

"Ffion's here?"

"She is."

"And?" Rocky asked.

"And what?"

Mum was being weird. Giving one- or two-word answers. Evasive.

"And what are you not telling me, Mum?"

17

Mum parked in front of the terraced house on their long steep street and opened the front door. Home at last, Rocky suddenly felt shattered as she followed Mum into the kitchen.

"Roy and Ffion are definitely asleep, I think. You know how he has to go to sleep by a certain time. Melchester orders."

Rocky laughed. It was weird that a Premier League footballer had a prescribed bedtime, had to eat meals off a list worked out by the club, had their bloods checked weekly to make sure they were living well.

The kitchen at home was smaller than she remembered. And she felt odd to be back in the house where she had always lived, having been away from it for three months. Everything looked smaller and old-fashioned. Different, but the same, too.

Also, it was now two a.m. UK time. Rocky had been awake for twenty hours. As she drew her bedroom curtains, aware it was colder still outside, she noticed that snow was falling. And settling. The garden at the back of the house seemed illuminated now by the snow. She could see herself down there in the garden with Dad throwing snowballs, rolling up the perfect snow on the lawn into a ball, larger and larger, until they had made a snowman. It was only after a few seconds that Rocky felt the smile on her face. She touched her lips. A smile. About Dad. A happy memory. Not a sad one. Not that gloomy feeling. She smiled even more broadly. Maybe being away from home was helping her in more ways than she thought.

THE NEXT MORNING, Rocky heard voices downstairs. Roy's voice. She flung on her dressing gown, still hung on the back of her bedroom door, raced down the stairs on a new carpet—she'd not noticed the night before as she was so tired—and hurled herself at him.

It was like running at a wall. He felt strong. Rocky stepped back and studied her brother. Tall. Short blond hair. A big stupid smile. That was Roy.

"Look at you," she said. "You're a man. Like a proper man."

Roy grinned. "And you look amazing."

Sister and brother eyed each other, both grinning now. No need for words. They were siblings. They loved each other. It was enough.

"He's missed you." A voice behind Rocky broke the silence. "He's been like a little kid this morning. 'What time is it?' 'Is Rocky up?' I think he's asked me that a hundred times."

Rocky turned to see Ffion, standing in the hall. Taller, too. More beautiful than ever. Her hair. Her make-up. Her... what was it? Grace? Calm? Gentleness? Rocky had always wanted to look like Ffion, Roy's ex-girlfriend and one of the main reasons she'd got into football herself.

But—wearing PJs and a pair of carpet slippers—she was clearly not his ex-girlfriend any more.

"Ffion! You're here! I thought you were in Australia."

"She came back," Roy said, gleefully, just as Mum looked away, avoiding Rocky's eyes.

After hugging Ffion, Rocky studied Mum, then Roy, then Ffion. "And?" she asked.

"And nothing," Roy said quickly.

"It didn't work out in Oz," Ffion said. "It wasn't right for me. I was homesick."

Rocky nodded. She got that at least.

"I'm back at Mel Rovers," Ffion said. "Player coach."

"Congratulations for that. But... but... I read online they've lost the funding from the club," Rocky said.

"We're back at the sports centre, too," Ffion moaned.

"What?"

Rocky couldn't believe it. For a few years Melchester Women had been building as a team, working their way up the leagues, funded by the group that owned Melchester Rovers. Now they had returned to square one.

"We've a game tonight, so long as we have enough players," Ffion said. "Come and watch?"

"Yes," Rocky said, without thinking. "Please." The idea of getting away from the house was good. She couldn't think clearly here. She still had this massive decision to make about her future and no one to talk to about it.

And, also, in the back of her mind she hoped that there would not be enough players and that they'd ask her to come on as a ringer. On the flight she'd been imagining pulling on the red and yellow of Melchester Rovers again. The fantasy had even included playing on the all-weather pitch at the sports centre. Like when she'd got into football in the first place.

18

THERE WAS A moment in the game—as Rocky put her foot on the ball and looked up to play a pass—that she realised things were different.

She was on. As a ringer. It was joyful.

When she used to play for Melchester Rovers, Rocky would have to battle for everything. Shoulder her way in to win a ball, tackle, foul to stop an opposition attack. Now—surrounded by high wire fences with the bright floodlights casting shadows onto the dark all-weather surface—the opposition were standing off. And her teammates were moving into space assuming she'd choose the right pass and play it well.

After ten minutes of the game the other players on the pitch—both sides—had worked out she was a good footballer. She thought of those players she'd watched on TV or at Mel Park who received the ball and the whole crowd slid onto the edge of their seats. The kind of player that made things happen, that you wanted to see get the ball, that other players stood off.

Was that really where she was now? Who she was?

In the first half Rocky played a contained game, sat deep and passed teammates into space. In the second half—seeing that everyone was tired—she began to make runs deep into the opposition half. Playing one-twos with Ffion, who was up front in a Kim-style role.

It was fun. There was no Abby insisting she keep her game tight, stick to her role. There was no coach other than Ffion, who seemed more than happy for Rocky to punish the opposition by doing whatever she wanted.

So that was what she decided to do, running at the defence, skipping over fouls, making openings for the other Melchester Rovers players. All older than her, but all deferring to her. Like she was some sort of star come home to her roost.

It felt weird. It felt good. But, towards the end, her mood changed from joy to gloom as she understood exactly what Ffion had been trying to tell her. Melchester Rovers women's team were moving backwards.

It wasn't that she had suddenly got a lot better at football, perhaps. It was just that the good players had left. Apart from Ffion.

The better players had gone, several moving

on to play for Tynecaster on the other side of town, a team you were meant to hate because you were a Melchester fan. And Rocky did. Her dad had taught her to. But Tynecaster were investing in their team. The Melchester coach had moved on, disgruntled at the lack of ambition at the club. And then everything had fallen apart.

They were back at the sports centre, no longer invited to play at Mel Park. So many clubs were hosting their women's team games at their proper stadiums now. Fifty thousand turning up for big matches.

But Melchester Rovers Women were here at the sports centre. And they didn't even have fifty fans watching. Let alone fifty thousand.

Women's football had made such gains, had moved on. But Melchester Rovers had not moved on with it.

The game ended in a 5–1 victory, but to

Rocky it felt like a defeat. If she was going to come home to play football in the UK, she couldn't play here. It'd be so depressing.

The thought that she could play for Tynecaster Women came into her head. They'd been invested in properly. They had a proper team, facilities. But, really, could she play for the team she had hated all her life? Wear their badge?

Ffion came over and hugged her. "You are class. Your game… I mean you were great before you left, but now… you've come on so well."

Rocky wasn't sure what to say. Should she gush and be grateful? Or should she be angry and ask what had happened? She stayed quiet, her default position if she was conflicted.

After getting changed in the dressing room alongside several members of the Melchester Marauders Fell Running Club, back from a headtorch fell run in the dark, and three girls who had been playing badminton on the indoor courts, Rocky and Ffion walked up the hill to Rocky's house.

Rocky wanted to tackle the issue. But how? How did you say to someone you really admired that what she was part of was really disappointing? Because she really did admire Ffion. Ffion had been her role model and—for a time—what felt like a best friend, someone who understood her.

"You're cross, aren't you?" Ffion made the first move.

Rocky smiled. Should she say? Should she spill the beans?

"Come on, Rocky," Ffion said, direct as ever. "Let's hear it. Or don't you do plain-speaking now you live in the States?"

Now Rocky laughed. Ffion knew her too well. She took a deep breath. She'd be angry about Melchester Women. Mask what was really doing her head in.

"Why are we back at the sports centre?"

"Money," Ffion said. "The Rovers board pulled out of the women's team. But they said we could still use the club's name. For now. But that's all."

"So why are you still playing for them?" Rocky said. "You're better than this."

Ffion shook her head. "I'm not. I was good, when you broke into the team. But you're miles ahead of me now. And I'm just not good enough to be a professional like you are. Not even a semi-pro. Just because I'm a decent footballer doesn't mean I can do any of that. You have to be excellent now. And I'm not. But you are. And that, my old friend, is very, very exciting."

Rocky felt a rush of adrenaline similar to scoring a last-minute goal. To have Ffion say such things to her. She drank it in. Praise from her hero. It was a big moment for her.

They were climbing the hill. She could smell the air coming off the moors above the city. She was enjoying stretching out her calves as she walked.

Silence between friends.

"Rocky?"

"Yeah?"

"You… you like me, don't you?"

Rocky stopped and looked at Ffion. "'Course I do."

Ffion suddenly looked emotional. Her eyes red and watery.

"Are you okay?" Rocky asked, putting her hand on Ffion's, realising it was a gesture she'd learned from Kim, something she would never have done before.

"Yeah." Ffion forced a laugh. "Just needed to check. For something."

They were outside her house now.

Rocky wasn't sure what was going on with Ffion. And with Roy. Was there trouble between them? Were they going to split up again? She hoped not. Were they even together? But maybe Ffion did have dreams of playing football away from Melchester. Perhaps it was time to tell Ffion about her own things. Fill the silence.

"I might come back, maybe play for Mel Rovers," Rocky said. "Don't tell Mum."

"You might what?" Ffion's eyes were wide. She put her hands out in a gesture of desperation.

"Come home," Rocky said quietly.

"I don't think so," Ffion snapped. Her face was fierce.

"Eh?"

"That's not happening. You are staying in the States."

Rocky shrugged and faced out down the hill to the city centre, lit up with Christmas lights, the green glow from the night Mum had driven her into town.

"Can I say why you shouldn't?" Ffion fumed. "Just so you can think about it."

"If you like."

"I do like."

"Say it then." Rocky almost wanted to laugh, Ffion was so vexed.

"Your brother will be the best footballer in your family. Your mum's heart will be broken. And I will be very, very, very disappointed in you. For ever."

Rocky wanted to cry. Ffion had listed three things she did not want. But she didn't cry.

19

THEY DID PRESENTS early on Christmas Day. Roy was due to leave Mel Park for an away day on Boxing Day in London, so they had to get through presents, a light meal and all the rest by eleven a.m.

As soon as she woke Rocky messaged Kim.

> Happy Christmas.
> Thank you. Still Christmas
> Eve here. Hope you get
> some good presents.
> Have a good time.

The front room was draped in tinsel and the tree was giving off that Christmas tree smell that—even if she didn't recognise it—made Rocky shudder with Christmas excitement. The four snow globes were in a line on the mantelpiece where they always were. And the old wooden and brush model of a reindeer was leaning against the wall there, too. It had three legs. It was a mystery where the fourth leg was. But they still put it up every year.

Ffion had stayed over in Roy's room again, so there were four of them in the front room.

Having Ffion there was good. Rocky, Mum and Roy would have been gloomy. It would have been all about Dad not being there. And it was clear that Ffion and Roy were close again and not about to split up.

Once they'd opened presents—Rocky got some trail running shoes and a guidebook to the USA—Roy stood up.

Rocky was about to shoot him down, mock him for trying to replace Dad by saying something meaningful and deep at Christmas that would only annoy her, but Mum shot her a look and she held her tongue.

Because something was going on. That thing. The weirdness with Ffion the night before. The odd vibe between Ffion and Roy. And Mum. There was something unspoken loitering in every conversation. What the hell was it? Was Ffion about to expose Rocky's plans to Mum? Had she already told Roy?

When it happened Rocky couldn't work out how stupid she'd been not to see it coming.

Ffion was standing now, too. And Mum beaming.

Rocky narrowed her eyes.

Roy began. "Mum. Rocky. Me and Ffion have got some news."

Here we go, thought Rocky. And her next thought was that Ffion was pregnant. But she kept her mouth shut. Kept a straight face. Or tried to. She knew that winding up her brother had to be done with more care when Ffion was around.

"We're getting engaged," Roy said and—as he said it—he reached out to Ffion and their hands touched.

It was sweet. Very sweet.

Mum jumped up at once and went to hug Ffion. And—as they hugged—Rocky looked at her brother who was grinning childlike at her, waiting for a reaction.

He got one.

Because suddenly Rocky was crying, leaning forward and sobbing into her hands. But why? What the hell was she doing? Why was she crying? This was their moment and she was crying.

She stood up wanting to leave the room so that the happy scene could go on without her, but her brother stood in her way and somehow she fell into his arms and they hugged and he said, "Are you okay?"

Rocky pulled back from the embrace and nodded, still sobbing, but laughing too; then sobbing again, she looked at Mum and Ffion, both crying now as well.

LATER, AT BEDTIME—when Roy was on the train to London and Ffion had driven home to be with her family—Mum and Rocky sat in the kitchen.

Rocky had just messaged Kim, Mahsa and Naomi to wish them Happy Holidays. Mahsa and Naomi replied immediately. Nothing from Kim.

"It all got a bit emotional earlier," Mum

said, interrupting Rocky's worried half-thoughts about her friend. She smiled.

"It's all good," Rocky said.

"It is?"

Rocky let out a laugh. She always found conversations like this funny. There were things to be talked about. Lots of things. But they were both just letting out words to fill the silence. Rocky laughed again.

"What's funny?" Mum asked. She looked ever so slightly irritated now.

"Us," Rocky said. "I mean… we're sat here saying nothing when we're probably both thinking how rubbish it is to have Christmas without Dad and that now Roy is engaged and house hunting he's nearly gone, and that I live in America and—" Rocky hesitated. Where was she going with this?

She looked at Mum, whose face was screwed up in confusion. "What is it, love?"

"I need to come home, Mum. I don't like it in California."

20

THEY WENT FOR a walk the next morning. Mum and Rocky. Rocky had still not heard from Kim. She was starting to worry about her friend. About their friendship.

High on the hill above their part of Melchester there was a tall monument called The Pike. Built of stone in 1815, it was about thirty metres high. You could see it from miles away. Down the valley, even from the motorway. It was like a church spire without a church and it was made of dark stone that turned darker when the skies clouded over. Darker still when it rained.

But this morning, after a night of rain, the sun was shining. Low and bright in the Boxing Day sky. The grass on the hillside was pale, almost yellow, starved of sun and drenched with water. But it was a colour Rocky liked. So different to the lush greens of the watered grass in California—or the incinerated grass that turned brown then seemed to melt into the soil when no one watered it.

They set off as soon as the sun spilled over the side of the hill. Up to the top of their road and across the moor where Rocky and Roy had played their first football and where half-a-dozen dogs now ran in frenzied circles, spiralling across the wet grass.

"Talk to me," Mum said. "You want to come home? Are you really sure about that?"

Rocky didn't know where to start. The path became steeper as they climbed. Rocky heard Mum becoming breathless and realised she was walking too fast.

Rocky had prepared reasons why she wanted to come home, as she lay in bed the night before. A menu of excuses to give to Mum that meant her US adventure could end. I miss the UK. I don't fit in. It's too hot. Even I am worried about you on your own.

"Rocky?" Mum pressed, catching up with her now, but still breathing hard because of the climb.

Rocky had always felt uncomfortable making up reasons for things that were feasible, but not entirely true, however convincing those reasons were, and she understood there was only one reason really. Why hide the truth? People knew the truth. The only person she was lying to was herself.

"I can't do the school work," she said. "I'm not clever enough."

Mum didn't reply. Rocky had expected her

to say Yes you are, love, and encourage her. But she didn't. They just kept climbing until they reached the top of the hill and walked— still in silence—along the ridge, splashing through shallow puddles that soaked the track, pieces of ice around the edges of the puddles as Rocky stepped on them gently to crack them on purpose.

Mum had not spoken for ten minutes now and Rocky was beginning to worry that she wasn't thinking at all, but was cross. Cross with Rocky. That would be worse than anything. She'd hate it if Mum was cross.

"I'm not angry," Mum began, her hand on the cold stone of the monument as she pulled her sock up inside her walking boot.

Rocky smiled. So her mum could still read her mind. A strong wind was coming across the hills now. Rocky saw a plane dipping out of the pale sky towards the airport.

"When I met your dad he was twenty," Mum began.

Rocky wondered why they were talking about Dad. But she never stopped her mum when she did so.

"He'd left school with three O levels—that's GCSEs to you. He had been unemployed and was skint. I mean really skint. And his mum and dad were selling their house, so your dad had to move out and find somewhere to live. A flat. But—without qualifications then—it was really hard to get work."

Rocky shook her head. "I thought Dad was clever. He was a union rep and—"

"Your dad was clever, love. He was just terrible at school. All through his school life he'd sat in the classrooms and it had not worked for him."

"I don't get it." Rocky was ready to challenge her mum now. Dad was the cleverest person she'd ever met. "Why are we talking about Dad?"

"Just listen," Mum said impatiently. "Your dad got forced to take a job at this factory. There was this scheme where you got a job and were paid peanuts for it. Called YTS. Youth Training Scheme. Something like that. And his boss, the union rep there, liked him. Knew he was good at his job. Said he had promised that he should go to evening classes. And study a BTEC. And your dad said no, he hated school. But the union rep said you only had to go to one class a week. For an hour and a half. That you had to teach yourself for the rest of the time. The man said if Dad stuck to it he'd give him a proper job, not on the YTS, and double his pay overnight. And he could have a half day off work—paid—to do the course."

"Right."

"So your dad did it. He went to evening classes. Rented a flat with his extra pay. Taught himself in the other evenings. Met me. Got promoted several times. And because he became a union rep too, worked his way up in the union to a really high level."

"That's nice," Rocky said. "I was proud of him, Mum. But shall we go home?"

"No." Mum shook her head. "You're not listening. Do you remember when you did that school project when you were about twelve? At the secondary school. And—because it was about football and designing a football kit—"

"For women," Rocky said angrily. "Because all the kits were for—"

"Men. Exactly. You were cross about that. And you worked flat out. At home. And nailed it. And your teachers were all over you. You won a prize."

"But that's it, Mum. The teachers were all excited, but it was nothing to do with them. I did all that not in school. I did it in my bedroom. I did it. School had nothing to do with it."

"Just like your dad, then," Mum said.

21

THE FIRST TIME Rocky, Mum and Roy sat at the kitchen table together to eat a meal—just the three of them—was the day after Boxing Day.

Rocky had given up worrying about Kim. She'd texted a few times and decided to leave it for now, until she'd spent time with her mum and brother.

The room was warmer than it used to be. Mum had had a new kitchen fitted, paid for by Roy. Like the carpet in the hall and the landing, like the new drainpipes and gutters. There were kickboard heaters along the bottom of the kitchen units and they seemed to warm the room up in seconds. But it remained a small kitchen with a table in the middle that made it tricky to move around the room, but nice to all be sat at the same table facing each other.

They were having sausage, mash and beans for dinner. Rocky had made it.

The kitchen blind had not been pulled down and the dark night outside seemed to be sucking all the light out of the room. Mum looked tired. And Roy had a face on. Melchester Rovers had lost the Boxing Day game. A frustrating 2–0 defeat away to Hullifax Town. In which Roy had had a bad game, the opposition defender not giving him an inch.

Before she'd left for the States, right back to when they were younger, Rocky had always teased Roy if they lost. From boys' league to park football. Sometimes it was funny. Sometimes it even helped Roy get over himself.

Now she watched her Premier League football-playing brother cutting his second-to-last sausage in half with his knife and fork and thought how pathetic he looked. His face. Maungy.

Rocky was aware she probably looked the same. She was still confused about what Mum had said to her on the hill. Still cross that Mum didn't seem to want to make her go back to the US.

Rocky had that sudden urge she'd always had—when things were unsettled or stuck in a rut—to charge in with a two-footed tackle above the knee.

This was her chance to break the tension. Perhaps to make it worse. But to break it anyway.

Rocky stared at her brother, willing him to look up from his food. "You know what your problem is, Roy?"

Roy narrowed his eyes. He knew what was coming. Some chaos. He looked away, then at Rocky again and sighed.

"Rocky," Mum said quietly. "Don't…"

"It's okay, Mum," Roy said. "I want to hear Rocky's words of wisdom. She says she's worked out what my problem is."

Rocky grinned. It was funny how they could revert to the same dynamic they'd had when they were kids. And how it felt just the same.

"You're a bad loser," Rocky said, feeling a rush of excitement. "A really bad loser. I watched your match last night and you were outclassed. You in particular. That Jean-Paul Camus had you in his pocket for ninety minutes. In fact… No… I won't go on… I don't want to hurt your feelings."

Rocky stopped herself and saw her brother was not eating now. A single sausage remained untouched on his plate. He always liked to leave a sausage till the end, so he could enjoy it as his last mouthful. She had known this fact all her life. And—today—she had been waiting for it. She had even chosen to cook sausages for this moment.

"Go on," Roy urged. "I'm keen to hear what you have to say. I've heard what the boss said and Match of the Day pundits. I've seen stuff online. Now I need your analysis for a complete set."

Rocky let out a laugh. "Well, according to my analysis, Roy, you were outclassed. They know how to play you now. You're finished. Dans la poche."

Roy smiled across the kitchen table.

"Merci beaucoup," he said. "That's great feedback. Anything else?"

"Yes," Rocky said calmly. And, subtly picking up her fork, she lunged across the table and snatched the sausage off Roy's plate and stuffed it into her mouth.

Now Roy was on his feet. "That was my—"

Rocky leaned back and began laughing. Hard.

She stopped when the contents of Roy's water glass hit her in the face and she heard Mum shouting at them.

22

AFTER WASHING UP, Rocky went up to Roy's room with a coffee she'd made with Mum's fancy new coffee machine in her equally fancy new kitchen. She knocked on his door.

"Yeah?"

"Got you a coffee."

"Come in."

Rocky went into her brother's bedroom. There he was, lying on his single bed, staring at his iPad screen. Still with Melchester Rovers posters on his wall. This Premier League footballer. This elite athlete. It was sort of funny.

There was still a hole under the mirror on the back of his bedroom door where—when she'd been angry with him, age twelve—she had put her foot through it. Rocky smiled. She was glad she never got that angry any more. The days of kicking and smashing things seemed to have passed.

Now she also noticed his room smelled. Like someone needed a shower.

"You stink a bit."

"Thanks."

"My pleasure."

"Is it poisoned?" Roy asked, sounding half asleep. "The coffee?"

"Yes, it is." Rocky peered at Roy's screen. "What you looking at?"

Roy turned his iPad round and showed Rocky the screen. It was a compilation of short videos of the French defender Jean-Paul Camus. Players beating him and not beating him. Hundreds of examples.

"Homework," Roy grinned. "So I'm not in his pocket next time we play them."

Rocky laughed, then stopped and stared at her brother, mouth open.

"What now?" he added.

"Like Dad," she said.

"Camus?"

"No. You. You're like Dad. If he had to learn something, he'd teach himself. Mum said."

"I'm like Dad?" Rocky had never seen her brother look so delighted. "Thanks, Rocky."

"You're still an idiot to me, though."

Rocky left her brother's room laughing. She was happy she'd made Roy happy. Making people you love happy was the best thing, she understood.

Just like she understood she had a call to make.

23

SHE WAS DIALLING the States even before she was in her own room.

One ring.

"Kim. It's me. I need to tell you something," she said.

"Me too," Kim said. Kim's tone of voice was deeper than usual.

Rocky hesitated for a second, then said, "You go first."

"Sure?"

"Yeah."

"I missed you."

"Me you. Sorry, it's been busy with Mum.

Busy funny."

"Busy funny?" Kim asked and they both laughed.

Because the weirdness had gone. She needed Kim. Needed her. To know that she liked her and that Kim knew the feeling was mutual.

"The thing I want to tell you... I didn't want to upset you," Kim said. "I mean... I know you've been through something similar, but this isn't the same... everything is going to be okay... and I'm worried this will bring up those dark feelings for you, so I've kept it to myself..."

Rocky wasn't sure, but she wondered if Kim was about to tell her about her mum. Kim had stopped speaking now. Rocky felt she had to say something.

"Is it your mum?"

"Yeah. She's ill," Kim went on. "But it's not serious. Like with your dad."

As Kim explained, Rocky felt stronger and stronger. Not happier. She was sad for her friend. But now she knew what was going on she felt like she could be there for Kim. Help her.

Kim told her everything. Her mum had found a lump on her breast. She had gone to the hospital. They'd removed it and the outlook was good. She just needed a few months of treatment.

"I'm sorry," Rocky said. "That's tough. Are you okay? Is she?"

"That's what I mean, it's not the same, not so tough," Kim said, a crack in her voice.

"Kim," Rocky said, trying to say it right. "You can't compare these things. It is serious and it is bound to affect you. It doesn't matter what happened to my dad. What matters now is you, your mum, how you feel."

"But—"

"I wish I was there," Rocky said. "We could talk. You could talk."

"I wish you were here, too."

"I'll be there soon," Rocky heard herself say. That was it. She was going back. There was no way she would not be there for her friend.

"You will?" Kim sounded suddenly much happier.

Rocky knew it was right. She needed to be there for Kim. To be her person. The person who could help her when her mum was ill. Or whatever life threw at her. Because she knew that Kim was her person. She remembered seeing it on a TV show years ago. Two women committing to each other. As friends. That they'd be each other's person. For life. It was simple.

"I will," Rocky told Kim. "I'm coming back. I'm going to be there for you one hundred per cent when your mum is having her treatment."

"What about school?" Kim asked. "You were so—"

"I will be fine. Naomi wants to help me, and Jesse said he'll be on my side. And I've got you. And—"

"It's like teamwork," Kim interrupted. "It's like you're doing what you do on the field, but this time in the classroom."

After the call Rocky sat on her bed and cried. First for her friend. For her sad news.

Then she cried about her dad. But not because she was sad about him not being here at Christmas. Or ever. She cried because she had had a good memory of him. Again. After nearly a year a good memory—something she could use to make herself strong—had emerged from the grief. She even had that idea in her head that she was like her dad. That he had struggled. But that he had emerged as a great person. Someone so amazing as her dad. If she could just be half as good as him, she'd know she was okay.

Rocky was filled with a new and powerful motivation. To be like him.

She could learn from her dad. Be like him and become the footballer she dreamed of being.

She walked over to her suitcase and unzipped the half with her school books that she had not even opened before zipping it up in her room in California. She had two weeks before school started up again. Two weeks to channel Danny Race.

24

THE FLIGHT TOOK twelve hours. Melchester to LA.

And—after three weeks of short days and long dark nights in England, the lack of light really beginning to make Rocky feel low—she enjoyed sunshine skies over England, then Ireland, Iceland, Greenland and the width of the United States for the whole journey.

That was one of the benefits of flying back against the clock. She wondered if you flew for a whole twenty-four hours whether it would be light all that time. Or if you could keep flying west and it'd never go dark.

Rocky had a window seat again. On the empty seat next to her she had a book and the iPad that her mum had bought for her. There was a maths app on it that guided you through how to do equations, formulas and the rest.

After her conversation with Kim she had sat down with Mum and worked out what she needed. If she was going to change, she needed help. Yes, from Naomi. Yes, from Jesse. But she also needed tools. Her dad had done a course online when she was younger. Her mum was doing a course online now. Maybe she could do the same. Find ways to learn online, away from the classroom where she never quite felt in control of her brain.

Rocky had already worked on the app at home in the days since Christmas and into the new year. Going at it topic after topic, problem after problem. And if it didn't work out and she scored low, she would do it again.

And again. Sometimes it took her a few goes. But she was ready for that.

She had done school work on apps before, but only ever to get it done as quickly as possible. And never to repeat it. But now? Now she would do it slowly, painfully trying to understand which number went where and why. Not just getting it done.

She also read fifty pages of the book they were studying at school next term. Wuthering Heights by Emily Brontë. She was enjoying it, so long as she read it in ten-page sections, then stopped. She couldn't concentrate for longer.

Once she had got over feeling angry about how the main character in the book was so mean, it astonished Rocky she was reading. That she was studying! Everything had changed since Mum had told her that Dad had taught himself.

By the time she landed, the three homework

assignments she had done on the flight no longer made her feel like panicking. They still confused her a bit, but she understood what she was supposed to do now. And knew that if she tried two or three times, she would get it right. Just like in football.

And that was enough. To enjoy it a bit. Not to feel panic. Not to feel like she was going to have to spend the whole term pretending she knew what was going on and dodging questions.

COMING OUT THROUGH arrivals, overwhelmed by the long white corridors and vast adverts looped on screens in every direction she looked, Rocky expected to have to get on a shuttle bus to the city alone, then another bus to the school. She could have called the school and asked for Joan to come and get her, but decided it was late in the afternoon. Joan would be home, with her family. It was more important to do that than pick up some English girl who had just flown in to study and play football at a posh school by the sea in LA. Whatever, Joan probably had better things to do, and it was easy enough to take a bus, even though it would take ages.

But, emerging from customs and border security, Rocky saw Kim waiting in arrivals. Looking taller, wearing a new coat Rocky had not seen before. A coat with a hood and a zip up front. She looked tanned, even though it was winter.

Rocky gasped and ran to her, hugging her. Then, slightly embarrassed at showing open affection, she stepped back.

"Hi."

Her friend smiled. "So how's new Rocky doing?" Kim asked.

"Good. I did some work on the way over. Read some of the book, even."

"Wuthering Heights?"

"Yeah."

"So you've been studying?"

"I have. I'm going to go for it. I can do it. I know that. I just have to do it my way as well as in the classroom. I am going to talk to Jesse about it. But I can do it, I know."

"I love you," Kim said, keeping her voice low. "I love you so much. Wait until we hit them with that in class."

Rocky grinned. "I love you, too," she said.

She wasn't sure what was going on, but she was looking forward to getting back to the school bit of Mountain Heights as much as the football bit. If she could just make sure she had time to work on the books and the problems by herself, then she knew she had a chance.

"It's great to have you back," Kim said. "I missed you. I missed talking to you. It was a bit weird… you know."

Rocky understood what Kim was trying to say. That they had drifted apart. Just a little. Briefly.

"Well, I'm back," she said firmly. "I'm here for you. You're here for me. Yeah?"

Kim's grin was wide. Her eyes were sparkling. Probably with tears, Rocky thought.

"So… how's your mum?"

25

THERE WAS A month between the beginning of term and serious soccer training for the state championship qualifiers starting up. In January and early February everything at Mountain Heights was supposed to be about school. About the classroom.

In football they would do basic fitness, and strength training, and drills, and work on plays. But otherwise it would be light. Like a rest period. Off season.

On day one Rocky went to see Jesse about school work.

"I had a think when I was back in England,"

she said. "We need to make a deal. Or I can't stick this."

Jesse put his hands together and failed to suppress a smile.

"It's nice to see you. Did you have a good break? And—hey!—you came back," he said. "I had a sense we might never see you again."

"Well… Naomi is going to help me. And… well, I'm an auto-didact now," Rocky said.

"Auto-didact. That sounds very fancy."

"You know what that is?"

"I might have looked it up for myself once or twice, you know. It's good to hear you using such rich vocab. This school must be working for you."

Rocky knew Jesse was teasing her. But that was fine. If he was making jokes, he was in a good mood. She wanted him happy.

"I need a favour."

"Okay."

"I need you to get the teachers to leave me alone in the classroom," she said.

"You do?"

"Yeah," Rocky said. "I mean… please."

"Leave you alone, like how? I mean… ignore you?"

"Ideally," Rocky said. She felt reckless. She was going to ask for what she wanted and not half-measures. "Yes. That would be nice. But, just so we all know what we're doing, the rules would be—"

"Rules? Would that be rules for the teachers?"

"Yes. Rules for the teachers."

"I'd like to hear those rules."

Rocky found the notes she'd made on her phone while at the airport to remind her what she wanted. What she needed. What she was going to demand.

"Ready?"

"Yes."

"One, teachers will not ask me questions unless I put my hand up."

"Doable," Jesse said quietly.

"Two, teachers will not stop me from taking notes just to take part in discussions. I don't like discussions, but taking notes helps me."

"Okay."

"Three, teachers will not comment on me staring out of the window: I'm thinking."

"Could be tricky."

"It's non-negotiable."

"Is it?"

"Yes." Rocky pushed on. She wanted to get through her wish list without being stopped. "Four, teachers will not stop me going on my phone: I'm doing research."

Jesse laughed, but didn't object.

"Five, teachers should just leave me alone.

Put me at the back."

"Fine. That's fine."

"And, six, if I don't show up, teachers should not punish me. If I am not there, I have an excellent reason."

Jesse waited to be sure Rocky had finished, then he laughed out loud. "I do think the world of you, Rocky. But you can see that all that's going to be tricky."

"Do I follow yours and Abby's rules on the pitch?" Rocky said.

"You do. Sometimes."

"Then that's a deal," Rocky said, standing up. "Take it or leave it."

Jesse laughed. "I'll have a word with Mrs Achebe and the others."

THE DEAL WORKED. As a result, January and February went quickly. Rocky felt relaxed about the classroom and spent weekday evenings with Kim, chatting and studying.

Sometimes they would talk about Kim's mum. Kim would ask questions, such as:

"Did your dad ever annoy you? Even though he was ill?"

"Yes and yes," Rocky replied.

"Oh no," Kim said.

"But it was good," Rocky said. "I always used to argue with him before, so it meant things were normal. I'd fight with Roy in front of him. He loved it. He didn't want any of us to change. He wanted life to go on as it always was."

Rocky hoped she was helping. She did her best to be honest and stay normal for her friend like she was suggesting Kim stay normal with her mum.

Kim went home at the weekends to be with her mum who was recovering from her treatment. Kim had decided to do all her studying Monday to Friday and devote all her weekends to her mum.

Rocky worked with Naomi at the weekends. It was good. Naomi understood things Rocky didn't and said it helped her to learn if she taught them back to Rocky, one to one.

Sometimes — just sometimes — Rocky understood something Naomi didn't and explained it back.

The teachers left her alone in the class.

At the weekends, Rocky spent two hours studying alone before football training, two hours afterwards and then two lots of two hours on Sundays.

She ate and chatted with some of the other girls in the evenings.

Then it was March.

And March meant two things.

One, the start of serious training for the state championship.

Two, the next school report, after the mid-semester exams.

Both could end up with Rocky being knocked out. From her footballing dreams. From being a student at Mountain Heights.

26

And—with March—Abby was back. The state championship qualifiers were just a month away.

So close. Rocky had missed Coach Abby. Even been angry at her for not being there. But that faded with the excitement that she was back.

Even walking onto the training pitches with Abby felt different. Jesse was great. They all loved Jesse. They were fitter than they'd been all year. Their bodies were stronger. Their touch and their technique were sharp after countless drills and skills sessions.

But—when they stood round the edge of the centre circle with Abby facing them all—Rocky felt an energy coursing through her that she'd not had since before Christmas.

And it was spring now, too. The air was warmer. The grass was greener. The trees leading up to the hills were leafing up. There was hope. There was expectation. There was a new energy. And Rocky knew that she was a part of that energy and that energy was a part of her.

Now Abby addressed them.

"We have one month before the two biggest games of your lives. You are fit. You are strong. You are technically the best you've been. You have discipline." Abby glanced at Rocky, imperceptible to everyone except Rocky, then went on. "You are all those things. But now we must become a single unit, a team. A team that can go somewhere in the state championship.

If you want it enough."

Rocky wanted it. She thought back to Christmas and how she'd considered not coming back to the States. How that felt. How this felt. And she knew she had made the right choice.

After warm up and drills, they played a game. Eight v eight. It was crazy, but they had not played a game, even a training game, for two months. Jesse had said it was to make them yearn to play football even more. Rocky thought it was because Abby was away. But she pushed her slight resentment back.

They played across the width, goal nets hauled round to be on the sides of the pitch. Rocky up against Kenzie and Kim in midfield. One of those training sessions where the coach holds up the game with one whistle and everyone stops where they are, so they can talk through the move.

It felt a bit like counselling to Rocky. Where you have to talk about an experience, then the counsellor stops you saying what happened and asks you how it made you feel and why you thought it happened. It was frustrating and annoying to stop to watch a ball you'd played forward to a teammate roll into touch when your team could have made it into a goal.

The first couple of times Rocky went in to win a ball—once off Beth, the other off Kim—she really focused on not going in too hard. She knew it didn't feel right.

The third time it happened, Abby peeped her whistle. Everyone stood still.

"What did I ask you to think about?" Abby asked Rocky. "About winning the ball."

Rocky remembered her instructions. She thought she knew which instruction Abby was talking about.

"Ensure every attempt to win the ball benefits the team, not me," Rocky said, hand up.

"Yes. But not that one. The other one. The last one."

Rocky screwed up her face. She was confused. She was starting to feel that pressure she felt in the classroom. That being on the spot. But she shrugged it off. For now. She'd process it later.

"Don't compromise your game," Abby said. "Be the players you are."

Rocky was still confused.

"Look," Abby said, sounding irritated. "To be the first Mountain Heights team that gets to the state championship we can't shirk tackles, and we can't shirk criticising each other. We will only become better if we can identify our weaknesses together and do something about them. Because it is not personal trying to improve each other: it's about the team."

Kim raised her hand.

"Kim?"

"Rocky's lost her bite," Rocky heard her best friend say. "Because, with respect, Coach, you've asked her to hold back from tackles. Be less brutal."

Abby was shaking her head. "No. I've asked her to hold back from foul play and vendetta."

A ripple of laughter ran through the girls.

Abby went on. "We need you to be brutal, Rocky. Brutal in the tackle so that no one on the opposite team will want to come near you. But this side of fair. Just like we need Ella to shout and boss the area so much she annoys you every second of the game, and like I want us all to know Mahsa or Naomi will get their head on a ball before anyone in the penalty area. Understood?"

The players nodded. Rocky looked at the ground and felt hot with irritation.

"We have to be able to call each other out and not be timid," she heard Abby say. "We need to challenge each other even more than the opposition."

"So can we challenge you?" Still smarting from being called out, still frustrated from seeing her pass run into touch, Rocky had said it.

All eyes fixed on Abby. Then Rocky. Then Abby again.

"You can," the coach said.

"Here and now?"

"Here and now," Abby smiled. "I am part of the team. If you've got something to say, Rocky, say it."

"Where have you been for three months? When we needed you. With respect."

27

"THAT'S A FAIR question," Abby said.

A silence as they waited to hear what Abby had to say. If she had an answer.

"Coach?" Kim pressed her. And Rocky was grateful to her friend for backing her up, being willing to challenge Abby, too.

Abby coughed. "I've been working with US soccer teams. A think tank. Developing ideas. There's a sense that some teams in Europe—Sweden, Spain, England in particular—are developing faster than we are. I've been helping make sure that we keep up."

"You'll need more than three months to out-think the Lionesses," Rocky joked, eyeing her coach. She had wanted to challenge Abby more directly, but it had come out as a quip.

Now Mahsa had her hand up.

"Mahsa?" Abby said.

"I think what Rocky is trying to say is that it was weird you just left and that you didn't say."

Abby nodded, glancing at Rocky then the other players.

"I see that now," she said. "I'm sorry. I was asked not to say anything, to be loyal to the USA, but I can see I owed you more. That I need to be loyal to you. Again, I'm sorry. If it happens again, I will be straight with you. Is that okay? Rocky?"

Rocky nodded, then looked at the other girls, who all appeared happy.

*　*　*

THE REST OF MARCH was spent increasing the intensity of training. Increasing the number of games they played. For the big ones. Two games that would determine whether—after Easter—Mountain Heights would get to play in the state championship for the first time.

More eight v eights.

And then scrimmages where they took on local sides.

In one game they played a school from New York that was touring California.

During the game against the New York school, Rocky went for everything. Hard, but trying to be fair. Winning every ball she went for with a tackle or a block and—working out she couldn't get the ball—channelling the opposition players away from danger.

It was good to beat a team from the east

coast. Rocky had begun to feel the rivalry between east and west coast. Even though she wasn't from the States. And the truth was the New York team were not very good. Ten minutes after half time, Abby replaced Rocky.

Rocky walked off the pitch frowning. She hated being subbed. Over the line and hearing the game restart, she felt Abby's arm go round her.

"Angry?"

"Yes."

"Good."

"Good?"

"Look," Abby said. "I want to see how they do without you."

"Why?"

"Stress test them. They rely on you too much in defence. You're my best player. And someone has to learn how to win the ball back and get it forward."

"They don't need that. I'll be there."

"What if you're injured? Or sent off? Or fail this semester and have to go home?"

"Hmmm," Rocky growled, still cross. But understanding what Abby had just said. You're my best player.

My best player. She belonged to Abby.

Best. The best. Was she?

She felt Abby squeeze her shoulder. "That's my girl," Abby joked. "I want you to hate me for subbing you. You're upset with me, aren't you?"

"I am."

Abby laughed. "But, listen. That performance was just what I wanted. You were aggressive, but you didn't get booked. That was control. Just what I need from you. On the pitch you have played a blinder."

"But?"

"But, you heard what I just said. We still have

to see how you've done in the classroom," Abby said, looking into Rocky's eyes. "That's just as important. I hope you're confident? Because, if you haven't done what you said you'd do in there," she pointed at the school building, "then this counts for nothing."

Rocky nodded. "I'm confident I did my best," she said.

28

THE ENVELOPE HAD the crest of Mountain Heights School in the top right corner and the following words printed on its cover:

Spring semester
report
ROXANNE RACE

It was Rocky's report. In an envelope, not an email. It felt old-fashioned to Rocky. But if that was how they did it at Mountain Heights, then that was how they did it.

What was it about seeing her full name on a

piece of paper that made Rocky cower within herself? It reminded her of school back in England and going to the doctor or dentist.

She knew her three closest friends had done well. Really well.

Kim was away for the day, seeing her mum. Out of hospital. On the mend. She had texted to say her results were fine.

Rocky had heard shrieks of delight from Mahsa's room and Naomi's room. She went in to see them. Congratulate them.

But her envelope lay unopened. Still.

None of her friends had pressed her for results. They knew not to. Nor had her mum. She knew too. Everyone knew how to be around Rocky and that Rocky would open the envelope when she was good and ready.

One envelope. One message. She would stay. She would go. She'd be a footballer. She'd be back home and not a footballer.

It was mad that something in an envelope that held your future could just sit there unopened and be a mystery and that all you had to do was pick it up and open it and the mystery—and your future—would be resolved.

As the light faded outside and the spring sun disappeared and the heating in the old building began to click as it kicked in, Rocky deliberated whether she should actually leave opening the envelope until after the big game tomorrow. Then—whatever happened—she could give it one hundred per cent.

There were two scenarios.

One, she had done well in school. She would be staying on as a student and a footballer. Everything was good and known.

Two, she had not done well enough in school. She would be leaving at Easter break in six days and she would not be coming back. And her future was unknown.

But there was something else playing on her mind, almost rendering this envelope meaningless.

Certainly less meaningful.

The game. The big one. The qualifier for the state championship. The envelope would have to wait. Rocky picked it up and put it on her desk and lay on her bed. Then she got up again and picked it off the desk and put it in a drawer and stood there feeling stupid. Then she pulled it out of the drawer and screwed it up and chucked it in the bin.

Still standing there, indecisive, her head spinning, anxiety starting to affect her physically, she knew she had to do something and picked it out of the bin and tore it open, removing a crumpled sheet of paper from inside the envelope.

Rocky Race took a deep breath and unfolded the piece of paper. She read:

ROXANNE RACE
Math: C
Geography: C
History: C
Science: C
P.E.: A
English Lit.: B

Rocky sat down on the end of her bed. She breathed in, her whole body trembling. These were the best grades she had ever had. Now she looked at the photo on her mirror of her dad, staring back at her.

She breathed out.

"I'm like you," she said to him.

29

THERE WERE THREE teams from Rocky's area of LA that had a chance of making it to the state championship after Easter. Only one would go through. Red Skies School, Green Hill School or Mountain Heights School.

Rocky was determined that that one team would be Mountain Heights. And so she approached the game as she did every game. As if everything that had gone before was over and that anything that could happen in the future was irrelevant. This was just about the ninety minutes. About winning.

In the first minute—after an early attack

from kick off—Rocky won the ball in front of her defence. Her first touch. She always liked to get her foot on the ball early. Feel part of the game. Touching the ball to one side with the outstep of her right foot, she looked up, ready to make her first pass. Then she saw another boot take the ball, felt her legs go from under her as she hit the ground and heard the ref's whistle.

What the…?

Rocky stood up. The stocky midfielder who had taken her legs stood up, hands on hips. Challenging.

"Hey, Rocky Race," the girl said.

"What was that?" Rocky growled. Her adrenaline was up. It was hard not to push the other player, put her down. She deserved to go down, didn't she? She'd put Rocky on the floor.

Then a hand touched her shoulder. Mahsa. "Look at me."

Rocky turned her back on her assailant and looked into Mahsa's eyes, aware that the other player was being shown a yellow card.

"They know you," her friend said. "They want to rattle you. They know you might react. Get a yellow. Even a red. Their game plan is to take you out of the game. Are you going to let them? We need you on the pitch, not scowling on the bleachers."

Mahsa held Rocky's gaze. Rocky heard the ref ask if she was okay. Rocky smiled. "Thanks, Mahsa," she said. Then, "I'm fine, ref. Thank you. And they can take as many yellows as they like. They're not going to get us that way."

Looking back after the game, Rocky would see that moment, and Mahsa's comment, as a turning point in her football life.

Another team had done homework on her. They had a plan. And she was part of it. They knew her name! And, because of that, she felt stronger than ever. Determined to do the right thing for her teammates.

For the rest of the first half, Rocky did what she always did. Played deep, passed accurately and broke up the opposition play. And there was a lot of opposition play to break up. Red Skies School were tough. Drawing Kim and Kenzie and the rest of the attack forward, then hitting Mountain Heights on the break with two wingers and two fast strikers. And that midfielder, hassling Rocky.

The game was probably great to watch with end-to-end attacks on the break. But for Rocky, more than usual, it was about that area of the pitch in front of the two centre backs, preventing Mahsa and Naomi from being exposed. Again and again she was prodded and poked by the two midfielders targeting her. The first fouler and another, a stocky girl.

To Rocky, they looked more like props in a rugby scrum than footballers to Rocky. Set up to force her back, bully her.

But after Mahsa's pep talk, Rocky was handling it. She wasn't going to rise to it. She wasn't going to get a yellow. Or a red. But she knew she might get an injury. The way they were trying to hurt her as well as make her react. Another hour of this, and there was a strong chance she'd pick up a knock and miss the next game. And that could not, would not, must not happen.

It was time to take control. Time to change everything. And seeing as Red Skies were cheating, maybe it was time she bent the rules a bit too.

The next time Rocky received a pass and the girl who'd been yellow carded in the first minute was near her, she began to run with the ball. At that player. Not away from her.

One touch with her left, then another with her right, she accelerated to make it look as if she was going to make a break with the ball into the opposition's half of the pitch. As close to the yellow card girl as she could get, she saw the knee come out before she felt it. It was just a nudge, but, because Rocky ran into the knee, rather than trying—as she had for the first thirty minutes—to ride it, she went down. Wanting the ref to see it as a bad foul, Rocky didn't roll around or make a fuss. So she just lay there. Played dead. For a few seconds.

Keeping her eyes closed, she heard a whistle, complaints from her teammates, then the referee saying, "Two bookable offences. You're off."

Result.

Rocky was about to smile when she felt a kick to her side. It hurt. She rolled over and jumped up, exploding with adrenaline and face-to-face with the second bullying midfielder who had clearly just booted her.

"What was that?" Rocky asked, feeling Naomi, then Kim pull her away from the confrontation.

"You diver," a Red Skies player shouted.

"Me? You reckon?" Rocky asked.

"I do."

"Who's to say?" Rocky winked at the girl.

"You're off too."

For a half second, Rocky wondered who had spoken. The voice came from nowhere. Then she realised it was the ref. The ref was standing between Rocky and the kicker. A second red card raised. In the kicker's face.

The fury on the second girl's face was overpowering. Rocky actually stepped back. Not her usual style. Something visceral in the other girl. Something dark. This wasn't a game for her any more.

"I know who you are," the girl spat as she was dragged away by her coach, who had come on the pitch to stop things getting worse.

"Really?" Rocky shouted, still flooded with adrenaline and rage, her head tilted upwards in challenge. "Because I have no idea who you are."

Rocky's plan had been to reduce Red Skies to ten players and get rid of her nemesis. Down to nine was a bonus. Now she'd last the game without a major injury.

And—even better—from the resulting free kick, Mountain Heights scored.

1–nil.

ONCE IT WAS eleven v nine and 1–nil to Mountain Heights, the game was over. Red Skies could no longer play deep and rely on the break. They had to come out. And two players down, they were easy to pick off.

Without the two terriers on her case, Rocky had time to control the ball, choose the right pass and even venture forward with short runs before passing. The opposition could only back off.

The game ended 3–nil.

Job done. Job one of two.

All Mountain Heights had to do was win the second game and they'd be in the state championship.

30

"WIN THIS AND we are through to the national championship," Abby said. "We are going where no Mountain Heights team—girls or boys—have been before. You'll be the best yet. The best ever."

The second match was not made easier by the fact that Mountain Heights were away from home and the pitches were uneven, the ball rearing up when you passed it fast across the pitch.

But Abby's pep talk had been good. Really good.

"I saw you take on those boys trying to

kick you off the training field last September. Lording it over you. I saw you, Mahsa, facing them down. You can show them today. That girls—at Mountain Heights, anyway—are more successful than boys at soccer. Am I right?"

There was a cheer. All the Mountain Heights players applauding Mahsa on.

Rocky put aside the complicated qualification route. The way the team tournament worked felt odd. Three teams play each other. A plays B. B plays C. C plays A. Then the team with the best record based on points then goal difference wins the tournament and goes through to the California state championship.

Mountain Heights were team B. They had beaten team A and now had to beat team C to qualify.

Simple.

Or it should have been. Because, with two minutes left, Mountain Heights were winning 1–nil and heading to the championship. Rocky and her teammates were about to be the best, to be able to go back to school and lord it over the boys.

Even with players from Red Skies being on the sidelines booing every time Rocky got the ball didn't put her off. It made her stronger.

Everything was going to plan.

Until it happened.

The thing. The catastrophe. The disaster.

In what was going to be one of the last plays of the game, Green Hill School won a corner, packing their attackers into the penalty area, their keeper even coming up to add to the aerial fire power.

Rocky ended up marking the keeper who was loitering on the edge of the box. As the ball came across, Rocky found herself under the ball, so she stood her ground, back to the Green Hill keeper, who tried to leap and get her head onto it.

Rocky didn't jump, for fear of accidentally handling the ball or being accused of elbowing the keeper. As a result she felt the keeper jump beside her, then fall on top of her. Both Rocky and the keeper went to the ground.

The ref blew her whistle.

There was a cheer from the Green Hill crowd on the bleachers. Rocky tried to get up, but the keeper was still on top of her. What was going on? It was like she was being held down, so she got to her feet and the keeper fell back down.

It was so confusing. The whistle, the cheer, being held down.

Rocky walked up to the ref. "What happened? Why is it a penalty?"

"Foul play, obstruction, number four. That's a penalty. And…" The referee put her hand into her side pocket. She was holding a red card. "And for arguing with me, a red for you. You're off."

"What?" Rocky couldn't believe it. "A red? For what?" She could hear the players from Red Skies cheering and laughing. She glanced over at them and saw the two girls she'd got sent off in the previous game. They were laughing, one of them bent double she was so amused.

Rocky was so enraged her head felt like it would explode. She could feel heat rising in her. Through her body. Into her face and brain and eyes.

And then she caught Coach Abby's eyes. Abby shook her head and gestured for Rocky to come to her.

Rocky swallowed.

She knew there were moments in life where something you did could change everything. And that choosing not to do that something was a way of making the future better. If she had gone over and attacked the two Red Skies players, how would it have ended? Badly. Who knows what it would have done to her, to her school's reputation, to all her teammates.

So—keeping her eyes on Abby—Rocky walked off the pitch, passing the Red Skies players, hearing them goading her, ignoring them and feeling some satisfaction in that. That she didn't rise to them. To Abby. To stand with Jesse, who put his arm around her.

Rocky realised she had changed. That she had control of herself. On the pitch. But in school as well.

"Well done," Jesse said, echoing her

thoughts. "There's no way you should have been sent off. But you reacted in the right way. You are doing so much the right way. I couldn't be prouder of you."

"Thanks," Rocky said as she watched the penalty shot fly past Ella and into the net.

The game ended 1–1.

Mountain Heights were no longer sure of making the state championship finals because now they had to rely on Red Skies not losing by three goals or more to Green Hills, even though Red Skies were already out of it.

Rocky wondered if Red Skies would lose 4–0 on purpose, just to spite her. She glanced at her two enemies and saw they were still laughing.

31

ROCKY HAD NEVER watched a game of football between two other teams that had a direct influence on her sporting future. Would she and her teammates get into the actual California state championship? Or not? She had no idea. And—to make it worse—she could do nothing about it. Her feet were twitching and she felt really uncomfortable in her body.

Green Hills had to beat Red Skies by four goals to go through to the state championship and prevent Mountain Heights from going through.

It was agony. It was horrible.

Such a big score seemed unlikely. Four-nils and five-ones were rare in football at this level. These were the better teams in this part of California. Equally matched. But sitting on the benches at the side of the pitch, Rocky and her teammates, under strict orders from the ref not to make any noise, watched Red Skies concede two by half time and, early in the second half, a third.

3–0. The nightmare was closing in. One more goal for Green Hills and Rocky's dream was over.

Now she made the mistake of glancing at the subs bench for Red Skies. There sat the two girls she had had sent off. Both smiling and waving, glad their team was losing without them, glad too that Rocky's dream was looking shaky. They were goading her. She twitched again, but remained sitting. Mainly because Kim had her arm round Rocky for the whole game.

"You okay?" Kim asked.

"Mmmm," Rocky managed to say. She was right on the edge of going over and having a word.

"You don't want to do that," Kim said.

"Do what?"

"Go over and… you know…"

"You reading my mind?"

"I can feel it in your body," Kim said calmly. "Your shoulders are rigid. Just stay calm, yeah?"

Rocky nodded. She understood what Kim was saying. She agreed. She liked Kim's arm being round her.

Until Green Hills won a penalty after a stupid clumsy foul by a Red Skies defender. In the area. So clumsy and stupid and obvious it looked to Rocky as if she had done it on purpose.

Penalty.

This was a stitch up.

"No." Rocky stood up, Kim's arm falling away. "No no no." She avoided looking at her two nemeses on the other side of the pitch. Then back at the player who had been fouled, who was receiving treatment from her team medic.

Rocky would not be able to stand this. She knew. The scoreboard read 3–0, but soon it would read 4–0 and the dream would be dead.

"I have to go," Rocky told Kim. "I'll lose it if they score. If we're out, I can't… I don't…"

"Want me to come?" Kim offered.

Rocky shook her head and descended the small stand of benches. "See you after." And then she jogged away, across an adjacent pitch, towards some trees, where she turned to watch the game through the stands and the people sitting on them. She dropped to her knees.

And watched. This moment. This moment that defined the rest of the school soccer year for Rocky and her teammates.

It was hard to make out what happened next.

From what she could see, the penalty was taken, then there was a cheer, then the ball was in play and there wasn't a restart.

What did that mean? Had the penalty been missed? It must have. Then Rocky saw her teammates on their feet as the bodies of players—both teams, one white, one blue— were all streaming to the other end of the pitch.

A counterattack? It must be. The penalty must have been saved. Or hit the woodwork.

Suddenly Rocky saw arms in the air. Her teammates standing as a bunch, then one figure leaving the group and running towards her. Now the Green Hills players were celebrating and the Red Skies team were slumped on the field.

Rocky glanced at the scoreboard. She read 3–1, not 4–0, just as the figure coming towards her reached her and hugged her.

"It's 3–1. We're through! We won the group! Rocky?" Kim was crying. Happy crying. "We're in the state championship!"

32

THEY SET OUT after dinner. The days were longer now that summer was coming, so there was time to go for a run and still be out after eight in the evening.

Two of them. So they could feel safe. Rocky knew she had achieved a lot this term. In the classroom, on the pitch, within herself. She still had to solve the problem of girls and young women not being able to go for a run on their own. Still thought a curfew for men in the evenings was a good idea.

It was still warm and the light was a mild yellowy orange as they ran. Slow running.

Recovery running. Working their muscles gently so that blood flowed through them and they wouldn't stiffen, especially, Rocky thought, as she had a long flight to Melchester coming up. Your legs could tighten up on a flight. You were more likely to get an injury.

A figure appeared ahead of them. Running too.

"It's Cody. You know the football—I mean catch player," Kim said. "Hey, Cody."

Cody looked round and waved as the two girls accelerated past him.

"Great football game," Cody called out. "I came to watch. Well done."

Rocky waved and shouted back to thank him. Then she was focusing on her running again. Because, for Rocky, the run was also about relaxing her brain. After all the pressure and intensity, she needed calm and clear thought, to get away from the post-match excitement and adrenaline. Forget other people. Even catch-a-ball Cody.

Rocky frowned as they reached the top of a long climb. She was going home again. And a question came to her.

Did she even want to go home, to get on the plane?

Catching up, Kim stopped when they reached a bench that looked out over the city one way and out to sea the other. She had one hand on her knee and was rubbing the side of her lower thigh.

"Strain?" Rocky asked.

"From the game," Kim said. "It's fine. I wish you weren't going home."

Kim's words spilled out quickly. Rocky slumped onto the ground to stretch. She had the feeling that that same idea had been in her head, but that, even though it had not come to the surface, the idea was there anyway.

Not to go home.

"Me too," she said. "I think."

"My mom starts her next phase of treatment this week," Kim went on. "In the hospital. My dad was supposed to be having me in New York, but he's made some dumb excuse and let her down, so I'm staying in the beach house."

"Alone?"

"Well, my grandmother's coming to look after me, but she'll spend most of the time painting. She's an artist. She'll be hidden away in the attic and I won't see much of her. And that's fine."

An idea occurred to Rocky. Not going home. Like, really not going home… She let the idea move around her head, weighed it up as Kim watched her, a half-smile on her face, but silent.

Why not stay in the US? Rocky thought.

Easter break was only two weeks. She could do some school work so she was ahead of the game for next term. Avoid the long flights. And be there for Kim. Why not?

Mum, of course. That was why not.

Her mum would be waiting for her, thinking they'd have time together over Easter.

"I'm being selfish," Kim said, reading her mind perhaps. "I… I just love spending time with you, Rock. And—with me not being able to see my mom…" Kim stopped. "But I'll be fine. I will swim every morning. I'll do some work. I'll see if anyone from school has stayed on. And go shopping. And just sit on the beach. "Maybe it's what I need. And I will visit my mom every afternoon."

"But who will you talk to?"

"You. I'll phone you."

Rocky nodded and stared at a plane that was rising into the sky over the Pacific Ocean, the noise of its engine faint in the distance. She couldn't get past the idea of living in a beach house in California without an adult to feel guilty about, with her best friend. For two weeks. She felt excited at the idea.

And then it struck her.

Did she have to go home? Did Mum need her? Mum had been saying all sorts of things about her life now, how she was doing better. She'd gone out nearly every day over Christmas to do something with someone.

What if... what if she raised it with her mum? How would that play out?

33

SHE WAITED UNTIL it was midnight UK time to call her mum. Four o'clock in the afternoon Pacific time. Mahsa and Naomi had already left for the airport. Outside, parents were picking up their children in large SUVs, heading off for a spring break in another US city. Or abroad.

"Mum?"

"Hey, Rocky. How did you do?"

"We won. We're in the state championship finals!"

"That's awesome. I am so proud of you. What a time you're having. You've done so well. Tell me all about it. Or do you want to wait until you're home?"

Rocky swallowed. Time to tell her mum the thing. Or to ask her mum about the thing. The thing being that she didn't want to come home. How would her mum react to that?

"So… Kim's mum's going to be having some treatment over Easter and I want to get ahead of my studies for next term and it's so lovely out here in the—"

"In the spring?"

"Yes. That."

"Then I think you should stay in LA for Easter," Mum suggested.

"Do you?" Rocky couldn't believe that Mum was suggesting exactly what she was hoping she would agree to.

"I do."

"But what about the flight? It cost money. Like hundreds."

"I can change it to another flight. It's flexible. It costs a bit more, but I always book your flights flexible. Just so you have a bit more freedom."

Freedom. That was a good word for it. Rocky did feel free. Free to do things she wanted now that she'd sorted out her school life and was in the right place with her football. But she knew her freedom wasn't just about her. It was about her mum too.

"But won't... won't you miss me? I mean, you'll be on your own."

There was laughter down the line. Then, "Of course I will. That's why I was thinking me and a couple of the girls could come for a few days in LA. I could use your flights. I can take you out to lunch a couple of times. You can show me round the school. Then you can get on with your work and not worry about me or Kim. And the girls would love it.

Because, although I love you and need you, I do have friends. We do stuff together. I'm doing better, Rocky. I've got freedom too."

AFTER SHE'D FINISHED talking to Mum, Rocky walked into the sitting room, where Kim was lying on the sofa, staring at the ceiling.

She touched Kim's hand. Kim looked at her.

"You heading off?"

Rocky shook her head.

Kim's eyes widened. "You're staying here a couple more days?"

"I'm not going home at all."

In one swift, twisting motion, Kim was on her feet, her face illuminated.

"That's awesome! Oh my God! So that's two weeks. Here. You and me!"

Now Rocky saw the joy slip from Kim's face and her eyes glisten with tears. "I was so scared of being here alone. And Dad was being such a jerk not having me over in New York. We can live at the beach house. Yeah?"

Rocky nodded. "All of that. But I have to study, too. I need to study every day. You've got to make sure I stick to that."

"I will. I'll keep out of your way."

"But we'll have time to practise skills and to get fitter and stronger. For the championship?"

"Definitely."

Kim stared out at the football pitches. Or the soccer fields. She looked like one of those characters at the end of a movie who is gazing into the distance because they have a vision of a better future. Of excitement. Of achievement. Of happiness. Rocky felt it, too. And, knowing that there was a hard road ahead, Rocky joined Kim and they gazed together.

Acknowledgements

I have really enjoyed working on *Soccer Diaries 2*. Amy Borsuk and Chiara Mestieri have been brilliant editors, helping me get the best out of Rocky Race and keeping it fun for Rocky and for me. Thanks, too, to Jamie Elby for his hard work helping Rocky find readers. And to Tamsin Shelton for an excellent copy edit. As with all the Rocky and Roy books, my thanks to Simon Robinson, who gave me a tough team talk after reading the first draft of this book. Necessarily.

About the Author

Tom Palmer is a best-selling children's author from Leeds, England. He has written dozens of books for children, including the *Football Academy* series, and continues to inspire young readers up and down the UK. He supports Leeds United.

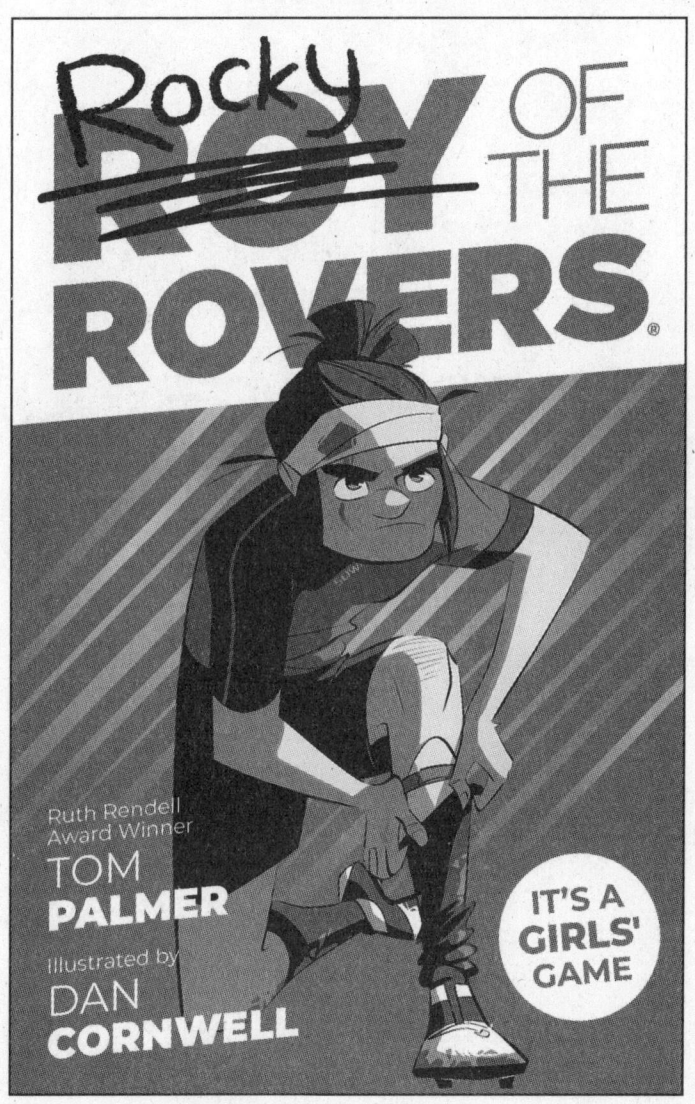

Book 3
COMING SOON